TYPO SQUAD

STEPHEN LOMER

www.stephenlomer.com

ISBN: **1546407626**
ISBN-13: **978-1546407621**

DEDICATION

I would like to dedicate *Typo Squad* to all the unsung heroes out there. That's right, I'm talking about the proofreaders and copy editors of the world. It's a thankless profession. If you do your job correctly, no one knows it. But if you miss a single edit, the entire world comes crashing down on your head.

Just know that I appreciate all you do, and I hope that you'll all continue doing it.

CONTENTS

ACKNOWLEDGMENTS i

PROLOGUE 1

CHAPTER ONE 11

CHAPTER TWO 31

CHAPTER THREE 47

CHAPTER FOUR 63

CHAPTER FIVE 83

CHAPTER SIX 101

CHAPTER SEVEN 117

CHAPTER EIGHT 135

CHAPTER NINE 153

CHAPTER TEN 173

CHAPTER ELEVEN 193

CHAPTER TWELVE 209

CHAPTER THIRTEEN 235

CHAPTER FOURTEEN 259

ACKNOWLEDGMENTS

Thank you to my wife, Teresa, for all her patience, love, and support as I continue on this journey.

Thank you to my fellow writers Christopher Valin and Chris Whigham for always having my literary back.

And the biggest thank you of all to Stacey Longo Harris, for taking this sow's ear of a book and editing it into a silk purse.

PROLOGUE

Dick was not a fan of math.

The quizzes in fourth grade had given him headaches and made him want to jab his No. 2 pencil in both of his eyes. Now in fifth grade, he found himself wishing for those fourth grade quizzes.

Mrs. Hitz was at the front of the class, preparing to hand out the test papers, when two men in dark suits entered the classroom. They asked to speak to her privately, so she stepped out into the hallway with them. Dick turned to his best friend Kenny and mouthed the words, *What's going on?* Kenny shrugged.

When Mrs. Hitz returned, she had a new stack of papers in her arms, and she looked anxious.

"Class," she said sharply, "today's math quiz has been canceled." There was a stunned sort of silence in the room; to everyone's knowledge, Mrs. Hitz had never not given a scheduled quiz. She began making her way up and down the rows, handing out the new stack of papers.

"These are . . . study aids," she said vaguely. "Don't open them until I give the word."

She passed by Dick's desk and handed him a booklet. It had a blank cover and a bright red seal on the right-hand side that read STOP! DO NOT PROCEED UNTIL TOLD TO DO SO. As Mrs. Hitz passed, Dick once again turned to Kenny and mouthed *What the hell is this?* Once again, Kenny only shrugged.

When Mrs. Hitz had finished handing out the booklets, she made her way to the front of the classroom. She looked everyone over, and then said simply, "All right. You may begin."

Dick used his pencil to break the seal and turned to the first page. It was a series of sentences, but there were no instructions saying what to do with them, no questions about them or lines to provide answers.

Just sentences.

Dick raised his hand. "Yes?" Mrs. Hitz said.

"Mrs. Hitz, what are we supposed to do?" he asked. The rest of the class seemed to be wondering the same thing, and waited for an answer.

"Just read what's in the booklet," Mrs. Hitz said. "That's all."

Looks were exchanged, but with no more information forthcoming, Dick settled in to read. The sentences were odd. He'd never seen anything quite like them before. They were mostly right, but there were commas in odd places, missing punctuation, and words that seemed out of order.

As Dick read them, he became aware of an odd feeling. It was a tingling that felt like it was in the center of his brain, and the more he read, the stronger the sensation got. He could feel his body getting warmer, and the tingling was quickly turning to dizziness. What in the world was happening?

By the time he got to the final page, he was deathly afraid he was going to pass out right in the middle of Mrs. Hitz's classroom. But he bit his bottom lip, read the last few words, and closed the booklet with a long, controlled exhale. He sat back and realized that his back was coated with sweat, but oddly, he didn't much care. He felt light and free, and as though he were glowing from within.

About ten minutes later, the last of the class had finished their booklets as well. Mrs. Hitz looked around and asked, "Now then—how many of you feel ill?"

Everyone but Dick raised their hand. His euphoria evaporated in an instant and was replaced with a sense of dread. No one was looking at him, but it still felt like he was alone on a stage and a white-hot spotlight had been turned on him. He wondered if he should put his hand up, too. Was he feeling the wrong thing? Was something wrong with him?

After giving the room a once-over, Mrs. Fitz's eyes landed on Dick. "You feel all right, dear?"

Now everyone *was* looking at him. He nodded nervously.

"Then report to the principal's office. The rest of you may step outside to the playground for some fresh air."

There was a loud scraping of chairs on linoleum as the rest of the class, all looking queasy to some degree, headed for the door. Dick remained behind, certain he must have heard Mrs. Hitz wrong.

"Mrs. Hitz?" he asked timidly once the room had emptied. "Did you say the principal's office?"

"Yes, dear," Mrs. Hitz said.

"Am I in trouble?" He hated the quaver in his voice, but he couldn't help it. It was hard to believe that only a few minutes ago he'd felt so blissfully at peace.

"Oh no, nothing like that," Mrs. Hitz said. "They just want to talk to you. Run along now."

Despite Mrs. Hitz's assurance, Dick felt his knees buckle with each step he took on the way to the principal's office. He'd never been there and had made a vow to avoid doing anything that would land him there. The stories of Principal Pade and his bellowing lectures were legendary.

When he arrived at the office, the door was ajar and he could see Principal Pade's desk, but the principal wasn't behind it. An older man in a black suit and tie was there instead, wearing tinted sunglasses even though he was indoors. Two younger men, also in suits and shades, stood on either side of him.

The man behind the desk spotted Dick and gestured him into the office.

"Let me guess," he said in a gravelly voice. "You don't have a stomachache."

Dick shook his head. He didn't seem to be able to speak.

"Come in; sit down," the man said. "There's nothing to be afraid of."

Dick took a seat across the desk from the man. One of the other two crossed the room and closed the office door.

"What's your name?" the man behind the desk asked.

"Dick," he said quietly.

"Nice to meet you, Dick," he said. "My name is Mister Flite."

Dick nodded.

"So tell me, Dick," Mister Flite said. "How are you feeling?"

For a fleeting second, Dick entertained the notion of telling him that he was feeling ill, that maybe whatever had affected everyone else had just taken a little extra time to affect him. But then what if he started asking specific questions? All he knew was that all of his classmates had felt ill when they'd finished the workbooks. But what if he lied and then offered up the wrong symptoms? It all flashed through his mind in a split second, and he guessed it showed clearly on his face.

"It's okay, Dick," Mister Flite assured him. "Just tell the truth. How do you feel?"

"Fine," Dick said at last, although at that moment he felt anything but.

Mister Flite nodded, and then turned to the man on his right. The man stepped forward and pulled out a small stack of index cards, which he handed over before resuming his position.

"Dick," Mister Flite asked, tapping the index cards on the top of the desk, "do you know what a typo is?"

Dick shook his head.

"A typo is a misspelled word. I don't imagine you've ever seen one before, have you?"

He shook his head again.

"That's because the government goes to great lengths to make sure no typos ever reach the general public. Do you know why?"

"No," Dick said, not sure what to make of all this.

"Because typos are lethal," Mister Flite said gravely. "Just reading a typo—one single misspelled word—can kill you."

Dick's eyes were wide.

"Sorry, I'm not trying to scare you," he said quickly. "I'm just trying to explain why you're here. Now, for reasons that we don't fully understand, there are some people who are born with an immunity to typos. Instead of killing them, typos have some sort of other effect. I knew a gentleman who would cry hysterically whenever he saw one. Another who would get a loud buzzing in his ears. But they wouldn't die. These people are very unique, and very special."

He glanced down at the stack of cards, and then back up at Dick.

"That test you took today was designed to see if you are one of these special individuals, and since those minor grammatical errors didn't make you ill, it seems you might be. But to be sure, I'd like to test you further. Would you be willing to look at these cards for me?"

Dick stared at the stack. "Do they have typos on them?"

"Yes, they do."

"Well," Dick said, his breath coming faster now, "what if you're wrong? What if they kill me?"

"Dick, trust me, I've had a lot of experience with this. I wouldn't expose you if I didn't think you could handle it. But if you really don't want to, you don't have to."

"I don't want to," he said automatically. His chest felt tight, and panic was beginning to take hold.

Mister Flite nodded. "All right, then. You can return to class. I just ask that you keep this conversation strictly between you and me."

Dick nodded and got up quickly from the chair. His hand was on the doorknob when he paused and thought for a moment.

What if he *was* special? What if he had this . . . *something* that none of his friends or classmates had? If typos were watched as carefully as Mister Flite said, he might never get another opportunity to find out.

Dick made his way back to the chair, taking slow, deep breaths.

"Yes?" Mister Flite said, raising his eyebrows.

"Okay," Dick said in a small voice. "Show me the cards."

CHAPTER ONE

The midday sun shone down on the lone figure standing in his waders in the middle of the flowing, crystal clear stream. He was casting out his line and reeling it in, but so far had no fish to show for it. This didn't seem to bother him, though; the mere act of fishing on a beautiful clear day seemed to calm him completely.

Behind him was his cabin, sitting on the rocky shore of the stream, and beyond that were towering pine trees as far as the eye could see. There wasn't another soul for miles.

He reached down and grabbed a bottle of Sierra Nevada Pale Ale that the stream was keeping cold for him. He took a long swig, wiped his bearded chin with the back of his hand, and placed it back between two small stones that were keeping it from being swept away by the current. He took a deep, cleansing breath. And smiled.

He could hear the familiar sounds of rushing water, tweeting birds, and humming cicadas, which is why he noticed the sound of an approaching car long before he otherwise might have. The tires sounded like they were struggling with loose soil and steep angles, and the engine didn't sound too much happier.

The car, a black SUV as it turned out, emerged from little more than a walking path nestled among the trees, then crested the hill, coming to rest with its front tires sitting on the stream's highest bank, a spot that would not see water until the spring runoff. A woman stepped out from the driver's side, slammed the door shut, and looked around. He could tell immediately by the way she was dressed who she was, and he had a pretty good idea of what she wanted. But as he was quite sure he wasn't interested, he turned his attention back to his fishing as she approached.

She stood there for a minute or so, arms folded, watching him, but neither of them said a word. At last, her voice carried clearly in the near silence as she called to him.

"Are you Richard Shonnary?" It was less a question and more of a statement of skepticism, as though she could not believe that he was who she thought he was.

He looked over his shoulder at her. "I prefer Dick."

"Some guys do," she said, without missing a beat. "That doesn't matter to me."

"Good one." He grunted. "Never heard that before."

He cast his line back out and reeled in a bit, hoping the conversation was done, but knowing it was likely far from over.

"You're not an easy man to find," she said after a time.

"That's by design," Dick replied. "I prefer the solitude."

"Doesn't it get lonely up here, all by yourself?"

He looked back at her. She had plopped herself down on the bank and was sitting cross-legged, absently playing with some pebbles scattered on the silt. Her bright red hair, pulled back into a tight ponytail, had turned to flame in the sun.

"See now, I thought that uniform meant that you were with Typo Squad," Dick said. "I didn't realize you were a therapist."

The woman smiled. "I *am* with Typo Squad."

"Well, good for you," Dick said. "Now if you don't mind?"

"Don't you want to know who I am? Why I'm here?" she asked.

"No, and no," Dick answered.

They lapsed back into silence. Dick could feel the young woman staring at him, waiting. The minutes ticked by, and still she said nothing. On the opposite bank, a fawn poked her head out from the tree line and cautiously dipped her head down for a drink.

"Oh, all right then," Dick said at last. "Make your pitch and get outta here."

"My name's Thea," she said brightly.

"Thea Saurus."

Dick said nothing.

"And a pleasure to meet you too," she said. "Anyway, I'm here to bring you back."

Dick looked over at her. "Bring me back? Back where?"

"To Typo Squad."

Dick laughed out loud, and the sound echoed over the stream. "That's a good one, sweetheart. I needed that. Haven't had a good laugh in ages."

"Tanka sent me," Thea said simply.

Dick looked at her thoughtfully. "Did he?"

"Yes."

"And why, I wonder, did Tanka not come himself?" Dick asked. When Thea didn't respond, Dick pressed on. "I bet he thought if he sent a pretty young thing like you, I'd be more easily persuaded."

Thea smiled again. "Was he right?"

Dick couldn't help grinning. "No. Now go away."

"Tanka gave me a message to give to you," Thea said. "If you weren't, y'know, cooperative."

"Is that right?" Dick asked. "Well, I'm definitely not being cooperative, so you may as well convey it."

Thea hesitated, then said baldly, "It's time you stopped hiding. It's time you got over what happened five years ago, you dumb shit."

Dick looked at her sharply. She raised her hands. "Look, don't shoot the messenger. Those were his words, not mine."

Dick's heart was suddenly pounding. He reached down, grabbed the beer bottle, drained it, and then threw it at a nearby boulder. It shattered into shards only feet away from Thea, but she didn't so much as flinch.

Dick waded quickly back to shore, dragging his nearly forgotten fishing pole behind him. He strode right up to Thea, who was a full head shorter than he, and jabbed a finger in her face. "You turn around, get back in that car, and get the hell out of here," he said menacingly. "And you tell Tanka to go fuck himself."

He strode past her, headed for the cabin.

"I can tell Tanka to go fuck himself, at some point," she called after him, "but I'm afraid I can't leave."

Dick stopped, looking back. "Why not?"

She shrugged. "My orders were to bring you back," she said. "I'm not leaving unless you're in the passenger seat."

"That's not going to happen."

"Then I'm not leaving."

Dick shook his head and spread his arms wide. "Fine. Do what you like. Goodbye." He stalked off toward the cabin, yanking the door open and slamming it behind him.

Dick paced back and forth in front of the living room's picture windows, trying to walk off his anger.

Tanka, he thought. *That son of a bitch. He can eat shit and die for all I care.*

He took deep, calming breaths as he broke out of his pacing and headed to the kitchen. He grabbed another beer from the fridge and was about to twist off the top when a bright flash of orange caught his attention through the kitchen window. His mouth fell open. At first he couldn't process what he was seeing, and moved closer to the glass to be sure of it.

Thea had unloaded a small, one-person tent from the SUV and was setting it up in a patch of grass near where she had parked. As Dick watched, she hammered in one of the tent poles and pulled the main rope tight to tie around it.

Dick shook his head slowly. He opened the beer, took a long swing, and muttered, "She'll be gone by nightfall."

But Thea wasn't gone by nightfall, nor was she gone the next morning when Dick went into the kitchen to start breakfast. He could see her sitting just outside the tent's flap, eating what looked like a Pop-Tart. She looked up and, spotting him looking at her, waved happily.

Shortly after noon, Dick emerged from the cabin with his fishing gear in hand and passed by Thea's tent, where she was still sitting by the entrance.

"Afternoon," she said. "Ready to come with me yet?"

"I'm not going anywhere," he stated emphatically, heading toward the stream.

"What happened five years ago?"

"Oh, all sorts of things," Dick said glibly. "Let's see, there was a presidential election. The guy with the hair won. That show that no one can ever get tickets for opened on Broadway. And the Houston Texans won the Super Bowl."

"Fine," she said. "Hey, is that water clean?"

"Of course it is," he called from his spot in the middle of the stream. "Why?"

She stood, dusted off her pants, and made her way down the bank. "My face could use a wash." She squatted by the water's edge and began scooping water up to her forehead and cheeks.

Dick cast off his line and tried to lose himself in the peace and quiet. He was just beginning to relax when Thea said, "So."

He closed his eyes and tried to keep his breathing deep and even.

"Did you know we studied you at Typo Academy?"

Dick's curiosity was piqued in spite of himself. "You did?"

"Oh yeah." She pulled off her black boots and socks. "They think of you as something of a legend there."

He snorted. "A legend. Hardly."

"Well," she said, dipping her feet in the water, "you did take down all those errorist cells."

Dick recast his line. "Yes. But I had plenty of help with that."

"Maybe so. But they didn't teach us about anyone who helped you. Just you."

"How long ago were you at the Academy?"

"I graduated last year," Thea replied.

"Jesus," Dick muttered. "Hey, if you studied me, how come you didn't know it was me when you got here yesterday?"

"Well, the pictures they have of you are a bit outdated," she said. "You weren't looking so . . . rugged." She gestured at her cheeks, and made Dick realize just how long it had been since he'd shaved his beard. It was a wild tangle, growing in every direction and streaked with sections of pure white.

"Oh." He stroked the hair, feeling its coarseness. "Right."

"Of course, the Academy's not the only place where they talk about the great Dick Shonnary," Thea said.

"No?"

"No. They talk about you at Typo Squad, too."

"They do?" Dick asked. At some point he'd turned to face her, and had completely forgotten that he was fishing.

"Yeah," Thea continued. "It's the same team you used to work with. Anna, Ewan, Big . . . they're all still there. They love telling stories about the old days. And you figure prominently in most of them."

"No shit," Dick said thoughtfully. "And you're working with those guys now?"

"I am."

"That's a great team," he said, and his eyes unfocused, as though he was looking right through the stream and at a movie screen of memories that only he could see. Then he came back to himself with a snap. She'd been lulling him, trying to soften him up so he'd go back with her.

She seemed to see the change in his mood on his face. "So why not come back and see that great team in person?" she asked quickly.

"No," he said, turning his back on her. "God, am I ever gonna be able to fish in peace?" he asked the stream.

"Is it still considered fishing if there are no fish involved?" she asked.

Later that night, as Dick lay in bed, his thoughts would not stop chasing one another. He thought of all the great times he'd had with Typo Squad, all the good he'd been able to do. What was he doing now? Hiding out on the top of a remote mountain, not catching fish. He did miss the old gang. And she might be young, but Thea was, based on their earlier conversations, sharp as a tack and, if he was honest, a laugh.

But how could he go back? How could he put it all behind him? How would he be able to do what he did before without always thinking about Chicago?

He stared for a long time at the dimly lit ceiling and didn't even realize that the soft *tap-tap-tap* on the roof was rain until it was coming down hard.

Dick threw the cover off, dressed quickly, and grabbed a flashlight. He stepped out the cabin's back door and squelched into the mud puddle that was already forming there. Slopping through the downpour, he angled over toward the little orange tent.

"Thea!" he called over the downpour. The flap unzipped from inside and Thea popped her head out.

"What?"

He hadn't really considered why he was out there. It just seemed totally natural to go and get her. To help. Maybe there were some things you really couldn't unlearn.

"C'mon, come inside," he said, water dripping off the end of his nose into his beard. "That thing will flood, and then you'll drown and I'll have to deal with having a corpse on my property. Less trouble to just have you come in."

Thea smiled. "Okay. Gimme a sec."

She disappeared for a moment, then unzipped the flap and came out into the rain. She was still dressed in her Typo Squad uniform, and it was looking a bit worse for wear.

"Didn't you bring a change of clothes?" he asked as he led her back to the cabin.

"I overestimated my ability to convince you," she said as she pulled her boots out of the sucking mud. "I thought we'd both be long gone by now."

They both stumped through the door and into the cabin's mudroom, drenched and spattered with muck. As they both unlaced their boots, there was a sudden, rattling crash of thunder that made them both pause and look up.

"Just in time, I'd say," Thea said gratefully.

"Wait here," Dick said, shaking water off himself. He went to the laundry room and grabbed a flannel button-down and a pair of sweatpants. They'd be enormous on her, but at least they were clean and dry.

He returned to the doorway, handing her the clothes.

"Oh. Thanks," she said, smiling.

"You can dry off and change in the bathroom." He pointed down a short hallway. "First door on the left."

Thea disappeared and Dick put on dry clothes of his own. By the time Thea emerged, looking like a little girl playing dress-up with her father's clothes, Dick already had a pot of coffee brewing. The rain continued to pound the cabin, and flashes of lightning lit the sky off in the distance.

Thea nodded toward the coffee. "Got anything stronger?"

Dick raised an eyebrow. "Yeah, sure. What's your poison?"

"Scotch. Neat," she said without hesitation, sliding into one of the stools by the kitchen counter.

"Suit yourself." Dick opened a cabinet filled with bottles of every size.

Once Thea had her drink in hand, Dick sat down across the counter from her. He sipped his coffee as they both listened to the storm rage outside. He noticed her staring at a wall covered in plaques and awards in the next room.

"Are those all—?" she began.

He smiled. "Yeah, all my awards from my Typo Squad days."

"Wow," she said, clearly impressed.

"Not that big a deal."

She slid off her stool and moved closer to the award wall. She pointed at a framed letter at the center of the awards and smiled. "Your school letter."

Dick squinted. "Oh. Yeah. Yeah, it is."

She smiled. "I have mine framed, too." After a pause she added, "We're special, you and I."

"Well, *I'm* special," he said, stroking his beard. "The jury's still out on you."

"Oh, trust me. I'm special."

"I suppose," he said slowly, "if I'm going to come back to Typo Squad, I'll have to shave. Be presentable."

Her expression brightened immediately. "Are you serious? Don't screw with me, Dick. Don't say it if you don't mean it."

"I'll probably catch the same number of fish either way," he replied. "So yeah. I'm serious."

Thea pumped her fist in the air. "Yes! I rule! I have accomplished my mission! I am the queen of Typo Squad!"

"All right, all right, settle down," Dick said, smiling. "You might not be so excited once you get a taste of working with me."

"Do you still have your uniform?"

"I do, actually. And believe it or not, it still fits."

"How would you know that?" Thea asked blankly, then dawning comprehension lit her face. "You've tried it on!"

"So what if I have?"

"You've been doing Typo Squad cosplay!"

"Oh, grow up," Dick said. "Hey, let me see your patch."

"I beg your pardon!" she said indignantly.

"Your Typo Squad patch?" he said patiently. "On your uniform?"

"Oh," she said. "I thought you meant—"

"Yeah, I know what you thought I meant." Dick shook his head. "Jesus, I'm old enough to be your . . . father's younger brother."

Thea made her way over to the mudroom,

where her uniform shirt hung on a row of hooks, and returned with it.

"I actually did have an uncle who wanted to see my patch," Thea said matter-of-factly. "He eats through a straw now."

Dick took the shirt, examining the patch sewn on the shoulder. It depicted the tip of an old-fashioned fountain pen on a circle of red, surrounded by a laurel wreath.

"Wow," Dick said. "Nice. I guess I'll have to get mine updated."

"Why?" Thea slid back onto her stool. "What was yours?"

"Oh, it was a bird of prey with a red pen in each talon," Dick said. "Pretty badass, actually."

"Maybe you can hang onto it for when we wear our throwback uniforms," Thea said slyly.

Dick narrowed his eyes and grinned. "Maybe I will."

The next morning, all indications of the previous night's storm were evaporated by a dazzlingly bright sun in a cloudless sky. It peeked through the curtains in Dick's bedroom and poked him right in the eye, waking him much earlier than he would've liked. He shuffled to the bathroom in his plaid lounging pants, splashed some water in his face, and looked closely in the mirror.

He examined his face from multiple angles. The beard definitely made him look older, but his icy blue eyes were still bright and relatively free of surrounding wrinkles, and the white that streaked his facial hair had not yet started peppering what was on top. All told, not too shabby.

He opened the medicine cabinet and pulled out a pair of scissors, a razor, and shaving cream. "Well," he said as his reflection tugged on his beard, "so long, old pal."

He came downstairs an hour later. Thea was already at the kitchen counter, dressed and ready to go. She had just raised a glass of orange juice to her lips when she got her first look at Dick and very nearly choked.

"Oh my God!" she sputtered. "Look at

you!"

Dick felt his clean-shaven cheeks and buttoned the cuffs of his black uniform shirt. "I guess I'm ready for duty."

"Oh my God!" she said again, approaching him for a better look. "Wow! If I had known what was hiding under that hillbilly I met yesterday, I might not have slept on the couch last night."

"Aw, that's sweet," Dick said. "And a little uncomfortable. Are you ready?"

She shook her head a bit, still disbelieving, and smiled.

"Uh . . . yeah. Ready when you are."

"Then let's get going," Dick said, "before I change my mind."

CHAPTER TWO

Dick stood next to the SUV, eyeing it nervously. He was really going to do it. He was really going to go back. Butterflies began to take flight in his stomach.

Thea finished packing the rest of her tent and slammed the rear door. Dick jumped a bit.

"All set?" she asked brightly.

He nodded. As she circled the SUV to get in the driver's side, he made a show of patting down his pockets, as though making sure he hadn't forgotten anything. In the right breast pocket of his uniform shirt, he felt the outline of something. He unbuttoned it and pulled out a few ancient index cards.

"Holy shit," he said softly, almost

reverentially. He flipped through them quickly, reading each one in turn, and felt all of his anxiety melting away.

Thea rolled down the passenger window. "You coming?"

He smiled easily. "Oh yes," he said. "Yes, I am."

Dick watched as the trees and his mountain retreated and gave way to suburban sprawls and paved roads. The movement was mildly unsettling; he tried to remember the last time he'd been in a car. Probably five years ago, when he was still with Typo Squad.

"Anna's going to be pissed," Thea said suddenly.

"If memory serves, Anna is frequently pissed." Dick looked uncertainly at the increasing traffic around them.

"I can't argue with that," Thea said. "But she bet that I wouldn't be able to convince you to come back."

"I'm not back yet," Dick retorted. "Although I do like the idea of causing Anna to lose money. How much did she put down?"

"Fifty bucks."

"And what kind of odds did she get?"

Thea smiled. "Two hundred to one."

"Goddamn," Dick said. "I would've taken that action. But yeah, she's going to be pissed."

"Ah, she'll get over it." Thea merged toward an exit marked DOWNTOWN LOS PALABRAS.

"Then we must be talking about a different Anna," Dick said. "The Anna I know is still holding a grudge from the time I emptied the water cooler bottle and didn't replace it with a new one."

"Oh yeah," Thea said. "She did mention something about that."

"Hey, how's Ewan doing?"

"Good," Thea said. "It's nice having someone with a British accent on Typo Squad. Classes it up."

"Ewan, my goodness," Dick said, ruminating. "He wasn't exactly a spring chicken when I worked with him. He's got to be, what? In his late hundreds by now?"

Thea laughed. "Could very well be."

"Hey, does he still talk about his time serving at Buckingham Palace?"

"Yes!" Thea cried. "Every chance he gets!"

Dick nodded. "Has he ever mentioned why that particular gig ended?"

Thea took her eyes off the road to look closely at Dick. "No," she said, excited. "Why, do you know?"

"Oh," Dick said vaguely, "one hears rumors."

"You have to tell me!"

"I don't know anything for certain," Dick said innocently. He looked out the passenger side window at the buildings and skyscrapers that now lined their passage. "I only heard that he had an affair with Princess Anne."

"*What?*"

"That's the rumor."

"*Ewan?*" Thea said, as though trying to wrap her head around the idea. "But . . . he's so *proper*. Not to mention old."

"Hey," Dick said defensively. "We were all young once."

As Thea grinned and shook her head, her phone rang. She answered it quickly. "This is

Thea."

"Thea, it's Autumn," the tinny voice said through the speaker.

"Hey," Thea said. "What's up?"

"The boss wants to know your ETA."

Thea glanced at her GPS screen. "About ten minutes."

"Copy that," the voice replied. Then, after a short pause, "Is he with you?"

"Say that again?" Thea said, and when she looked over at Dick, he was smiling.

"I asked if he was with you," the voice said, and Thea couldn't help but notice the slightly higher pitch and a bit of a flutter in the woman's voice.

"Hi, Autumn," Dick said, grinning.

"Richard!" Autumn practically shrieked, causing static on the phone's speaker. "You old hound! How are you?"

"For a guy who's been living like a hermit for five years or so, not too shabby." Dick ran his hand across his newly shorn face. "How are you, darling?"

"Still single," Autumn offered up immediately.

"Well that's good to know," Dick said. "I'd hate to have to duel your husband at ten paces for your affections."

"If it came to that, I'd shoot him myself," Autumn said, and giggled.

"Um, if you two are finished?" Thea said as she navigated through increasing midtown traffic.

"I'll see you soon, beautiful," Dick said, and before Autumn could reply, Thea hit the END CALL button.

"You and Autumn?" Thea stole a look at Dick as she approached a large intersection.

"Don't know what you mean," Dick said. "Just being polite."

"Uh huh." Thea turned into a squat gray parking garage. She found a space and threw the SUV into park. "Lucky for you, we're here. But this conversation is far from over."

Dick merely shrugged, a smile still spread across his face. "I'm only human, kiddo."

Thea regarded him with a sideways glance. "I'm starting to wonder."

Typo Squad headquarters was a shabby

two-story brick building next door to police headquarters. Dick and Thea passed through the outer doors and into a lobby, where a stout, jolly-looking woman with short blonde hair sat behind the front desk, laughing to herself. The woman looked up as Dick and Thea approached.

"Richard!" the woman shouted, bounding out of her chair and nearly leaping the counter to get to him. She grasped him in a tight bear hug, pinning his arms to his sides.

"I prefer Dick," he wheezed.

"Yeah, I've heard that about you," the woman said, and her raucous laughter echoed off the lobby walls. She leaned back, getting a better look at his face. "My God, it's good to have you back."

Thea sidled up next to them, smirking. "I'd ask if you remember Autumn Leeves, here," she said to Dick, "but apparently you two remember each other just fine."

Autumn finally released her grip on Dick and smoothed out his uniform shirt for him, taking her sweet time.

"Oh honey," Autumn said to Thea, "you

don't forget a man like this. You sure do miss him, though."

"And a man like this misses you too, sweetheart," Dick said, leaning down to kiss her blushing cheek. He looked briefly around the lobby. "This place hasn't changed much. Hey, do they still give you the confiscated typos?"

"Oh yeah!" Autumn said excitedly. "I was just reading one when you came in. C'mere—you gotta hear this one."

She made her way back around the desk, Dick and Thea following. Autumn flipped open a folder and began to read. "From a cookbook, okay? 'Add cinnamon, vanilla, and sugar, and stir in a small *bowel*.'" She burst into howling laughter, loud enough to echo off the lobby's marble walls, as Dick and Thea looked on, their expressions unchanged.

"BOWEL!" Autumn shrieked. "Can you believe that? A small *bowel*!"

"Good one," Dick said flatly.

Autumn's laughter slowly tapered off. "Oh, you're no fun. You used to be fun. *Dick*."

Thea snorted laughter and offered Autumn a fist-pound, which Autumn was only too happy to return.

"Well, anyway, welcome back," Autumn said to Dick. "The place was never the same without you."

Dick and Thea made their way farther into the building. They turned a corner and entered an open, brightly lit office area dotted with old, industrial-style desks. Dick slowed down and eventually stopped, drinking in the familiar space.

Near one of the middle desks, four agents in Typo Squad uniforms were casually talking: a heavyset man with a dark crew cut, an older gentleman with a meticulously coiffed mane of silvery-white hair, an intense-looking dark-haired woman with her thumbs hooked into her uniform belt, and a very good-looking blond man with blindingly white teeth whom Dick didn't recognize.

Before Dick had a chance to approach, a door on the far side of the office slammed open. A fat, sweating Asian man came through, holding a sheaf of paper. Everything stopped and all eyes were upon him.

"The mayor cut our goddamned budget again!" the Asian man shouted. "How the hell am I supposed to run this organization with no money?"

The other four looked to answer him, but he pointed a warning finger at them. "That was rhetorical! I'm not done ranting yet!"

The agents nodded and remained silent.

"I mean, look at these numbers!" The Asian man slapped the papers with his free hand as he began to pace. "What, are typos suddenly less deadly now? Can I just lay everybody off and hope that no typos make their way out into the general public?"

He had built up a head of steam, and the veins in his forehead stood out, pulsing. "I'm just barely getting by with what I have!" he suddenly exploded. "And if the mayor thinks I'm just going to sit by and let him slash a crucial service like Typo Squad, I will tell you this: he doesn't know . . ." he stopped as he caught sight of Dick and Thea across the room. Dick winked at the man and offered a jaunty wave.

". . . Dick," the man finished.

After a few moments of silence, Thea gestured toward the Asian man. "I'm sure you remember Lieutenant Tanka," she said.

Dick crossed the room and shook Tanka's hand. "You never forget your first. Hey, boss."

Tanka shook Dick's hand in a bit of a daze, as though he couldn't accept the reality of what he was seeing. Then he shook his head, let go of Dick's hand, and folded his arms in front of him. He turned to Thea. "Where the hell have you been?" he snapped.

"Hey!" Thea said. "You told me to go get him, and I did!"

"Why did it take three days?"

"Oh, he was ready to come back on the first day," Thea said dramatically. "But we decided to stay on the mountain and make passionate love out under the stars—"

"All right, all right, shut it!" Tanka barked.

"Shutting it. Sir," Thea said, grinning.

As Tanka silently sized Dick up, the other agents made their way toward him; the blond stranger with the bright teeth hung back. Thea gestured toward the heavyset man with the crew cut. "I'm sure no introductions are necessary. You remember Chris 'Big' Whig?"

Chris and Dick grabbed one another in a fierce hug. "Hey, Big," Dick said with a grin. "You look like a million bucks."

"Only if they're paying by the pound," Big said. "Good to have you back, my man."

The men released one another and Thea nodded toward the older man. "And Ewan Hoozarmi?"

Ewan shook Dick's hand and offered a small bow. "Having you back here is just like old times," Ewan said in a clipped British accent.

"Every time with you is old times," Big offered.

Ewan ignored him, nodding his head toward Thea. "Can you believe how young they are now? I daresay I was a member of Typo Squad before she was born."

"You were a member of Typo Squad before *everyone* was born," Big said.

Ewan turned to Big. "Christopher, as I

have told you on numerous occasions, I refuse to engage your juvenile banter. On a related note, I engaged in intercourse with your mother last night, and must express my profound disappointment."

Big laughed. "You have the most proper insults I've ever heard, you know that?"

"And of course," said Thea, nodding toward the dark-haired woman, "Anna Flaxis."

Anna approached Dick, unhooked her thumbs from her belt, and slapped him hard across the face.

"You lost me a bet, you son of a bitch," she said. They stared into each other's eyes for a moment, then Anna smiled, threw her arms around Dick's neck, and kissed him hard on the mouth.

Thea turned to Big. "Jesus. Her too?"

"Now that Dick's back, that's a phrase you're going to be saying a lot," Big said. He leveled a gaze at her. "*A lot*."

Anna released Dick from her embrace. "Welcome back," she said gruffly.

The blond man finally made his way over.

His arms were crossed and he had a cocksure sneer on his face, to which Dick took an instant dislike. The man took a few moments to look Dick up and down, and then his sneer turned to a smirk as he at last held out his hand.

"Scott Shwiski," he said, aggressively grabbing Dick's hand and squeezing tighter than was necessary. "Typo Squad field commander." Dick squeezed back, but when he let go, Scott held on. "I wasn't aware that we were in the business of teaching old dogs new tricks," he said.

Dick stared at Scott as an uncomfortable silence filled the room. He took back his hand and smiled. "Well, see, the great thing about old dogs is that we're well-trained," Dick said. "The problem with pups is that they're always pissing all over the floor. Oh, and they're all bark and no bite."

Scott's expression turned thunderous. Dick turned away from him and addressed the rest of the team. "Well, thanks to most of you for that warm reception." Dick looked around. "So. What now?"

Tanka approached and thumbed the old insignia on Dick's uniform sleeve. "Old school may be popular these days," he said, "but you're out of uniform, Agent Shonnary."

"Same ol' Tanka," Dick said. "Hey, it's weird that this is just occurring to me. I've known you for, what, twenty years now? Do you *have* a first name?"

"No," said Tanka simply.

Dick paused for elaboration.

"Do you have a last name, then?" Dick pressed.

"No."

"So you're just Tanka?"

"Just Tanka."

"And you never considered a career as a pop star?" Dick asked.

"When I'm stuck in conversations like this, I do regret my career choice," Tanka said. He picked up the budget paperwork from a nearby desk. "Oh yes—and when I have to deal with bullshit."

"Hey, if I'm not in the budget, I'll go back to my cabin on the mountain and resume my career as the world's worst fisherman," Dick said.

"He really is pretty bad," Thea interjected.

"After it took this long to get you back to civilization?" Tanka asked. "Not on your life. Get a new uniform and meet us on the range in half an hour."

CHAPTER THREE

The Typo Squad shooting range occupied the entire basement floor of the headquarters building. At one end was the armory; at the other were paper targets that approximated the human form.

Dick finished buttoning his new uniform shirt as he and Thea arrived at the range's outer door. Tanka, Big, Ewan, Scott, and Anna were waiting for them.

"Lookin' good," Big said. "Black really is your color, Dick."

"They say black is slimming," Ewan said, eyeing Big. "Of course, they say a lot of things."

"Oh, good one, Ewan," Big said. "Hey, how exciting was it to carve the face on the

Sphinx?"

"Nearly as exciting as suckling on your mother's teats when you were finished with them," Ewan replied, not skipping a beat. "Nearly."

"Knock it off, the both of you," Tanka growled. "Are you ready?" he asked Dick.

"Let's find out." Dick followed as Tanka swung open the heavy steel door that led to the range.

Dick was surprised to find the range already occupied. Standing near the firing stalls was a tall, skinny man with a prominent nose and tight black goatee. He was speaking quietly with three young recruits, easily spotted by their red uniforms and caps.

Dick wasted no time in sneaking up behind the man. "Well, well, well," Dick said loudly, and the man jumped. "If it isn't my old friend, Justin Case."

A huge smile spread across Justin's face, revealing two rows of crooked teeth. "Dick Shonnary!" he cried, grabbing Dick's outstretched hand and pumping it enthusiastically. "What're you doing here?"

"Haven't you heard?" he smiled. "I'm back on the team."

"Provisionally," Scott called from a distance. Everyone ignored him.

"Wow," Justin said. "Wow. Well welcome back."

Dick turned his attention to the recruits: a dark-haired kid with glasses, a teenage girl with piercing blue eyes, and a gangly redhead boy. They were regarding Dick with a mixture of awe and fear.

Dick looked over his shoulder at Thea. "And I thought *you* looked young."

"I *am* young," Thea replied.

The kid with the glasses swallowed hard and seemed to find his voice. "Are you . . . are you *the* Dick Shonnary?" he asked timidly.

"Yes," Dick replied simply.

"Wow," he heard the redheaded boy say under his breath.

Dick turned to Justin. "Do you mind if I take over for a minute?"

Justin smiled and spread his arms wide. "By all means."

Dick clasped his hands behind his back

and regarded the three young people in front of him. "What, cadets don't stand at attention anymore?"

The three of them immediately slapped their arms tight by their sides, stood up straight, and puffed their chests out, staring straight ahead.

"You," Dick said to the dark-haired boy, starting to pace back and forth in front of them. "What is Typo Squad?"

"Typo Squad is a division of law enforcement charged with protecting the general public from typographical errors," the boy said quickly. "Sir."

Dick stopped in front of the girl. "And why does the general public need protecting from typographical errors?" he asked.

"Because typographical errors are fatal to ninety-eight percent of the population," the girl replied. "Sir."

"And what about the other two percent to whom typographical errors are not fatal?" he asked the red-haired boy.

"They join Typo Squad," the boy said with a proud smile. "Or the Civilian Language

Inspection Team."

"And how do we more commonly refer to members of the Civilian Language Inspection Team?"

The boy turned slightly pink in the cheeks. "CLITs."

Dick turned to Justin and gave an appreciative nod. Justin returned the gesture.

"And those who do join Typo Squad or the CLITs," Dick said, returning to the first boy. "How do typos affect them?"

"With tics, sir."

"And what is a tic?"

"It's a physiological response upon encountering a typo," the boy said. "Each person's tic is unique."

"And what is your tic, son?"

The boy's eyes grew wide. He looked over at Justin, who nodded as he mouthed the words *It's okay.*

"I get a terrible nosebleed whenever I see a typo," the boy said quietly. "Sir."

Dick turned to the girl. "And you?"

The girl paused, and then said haltingly, "Typos cause my legs to go numb, sir."

Dick blinked at her for a long few moments. "That's going to be a tough one to manage," he said kindly.

The girl looked at him. "Yes, sir."

"You'll manage," Dick said with a small pat on her arm. The girl blushed, smiling.

He moved on the redheaded boy. "And you?"

The boy looked at his feet. "I'd really rather not say," he mumbled.

"Come on now, son," Dick said. "Everyone in this room has one. There's no reason to be embarrassed."

The boy looked up at Dick, suddenly defiant. "Typos cause me to wet myself."

Dick's expression remained set. He leaned close to the boy. "Kid, believe me when I tell you this: I have seen much worse tics than that."

The boy's face brightened. "Really?"

"Much worse," Dick repeated. "You're gonna be all right."

Dick took a step backward, regarding all three of them. He spread his arms wide and said, "Now who can tell me why this is the most important room in the entire Typo Squad organization?"

The cadets looked at one another helplessly. They clearly hadn't gotten to that point in their training.

"Because," Dick said, "this is where you train to use your weapon while managing your tics."

He pointed to the far side of the range. "You see those targets down there? When the range is active, a card with a typo will drop down into your field of vision. It'll activate your tic, and you'll learn to take your shots while it's happening."

He turned back to his crew. "Hey Big, c'mere. Show them what I mean."

Scott stepped in front of Big, blocking his way. "Sorry, old timer," he said. "I give the orders around here."

"Shut your hole, Shwiski," Tanka growled. "Big, go ahead."

Big trotted over. "I get to shoot stuff now?" he asked.

"Yeah," Dick said. "Show 'em how it's done."

Big stepped up to the nearest shooting stall. He put on ear and eye protection, then unholstered his sidearm.

"Active range!" Justin called out, flipping a large switch near the door. A Klaxon sounded and twirling yellow lights flashed along the ceiling. Dick gathered up the three cadets and pointed to a sign on the left-hand wall that read ALL NON-ACTIVE SHOOTERS LOOK HERE.

"It's so you don't have to deal with your tic while watching someone else shoot," Dick explained. So no one was watching Big on the range, but they could hear him.

Bang!

"Fuck!" Big shouted.

Bang!

"Cunt waffle!"

Bang!

"Prick flaps!"

Bang!

"Nut bucket!"

Bang!

"Cock bunker!"

A silence fell over the range and remained

unbroken until Big shouted, "Clear!" Dick, Tanka, Thea, Anna, Justin, and the three cadets crowded Big's shooting stall, while Scott remained in the background.

"God, I've missed your tic," Dick said as Big pressed the button to retrieve his target.

"I never know what's going to come out," Big said, "but y'know, I think 'nut bucket' might be my new favorite."

"Oh, I don't know," Thea piped up. "I think 'cunt waffle' could be a contender."

Big unhooked the target and handed it to Dick, who displayed it for the cadets. Three perfect head shots, and two in the chest.

"See that?" asked Dick. "Big curses uncontrollably with his tic, and he can still pull shots like these. You guys will, too."

The female cadet timidly raised her hand.

"Yes?" Dick asked.

"Um . . . I wondered if we might see you shoot," she said quietly. "Sir."

Dick looked from the girl to the rest of his team. Tanka shrugged.

"I'm sure you could use the practice," Scott said waspishly. Again, he was roundly ignored.

"Go ahead, Dick," Anna said. "Shake off that hermit rust."

Dick looked at her. "Hermit rust?"

"Well, you weren't shooting the fish, were you?"

"To be fair, he wasn't catching them either," said Thea.

"All right, all right," Dick said. "I'll take some shots."

He stepped up to the shooting stall and put on the protective gear. As he unholstered his weapon, he saw the yellow lights flash and heard the Klaxon and a very muffled Justin call out that the range was active.

As he lined up his shot to the dead center of the target's head, a sign swung down from the ceiling and into his field of vision. In bold black letters against a white background was the word THIER.

He felt it immediately. A warm sensation that seemed to bloom from the center of his brain, numbing his senses and making the world go hazy. An easy, lopsided grin came to his face and he felt his shoulder collide with the side of the shooting stall. He thought he heard voices calling from behind him, but with the ear protection he couldn't be certain.

The gun didn't want to cooperate and neither did his eyes, but he lined up the shot as best he could and fired off several rounds. Justin called that the range was clear, and Dick suddenly felt hands on his arms and shoulders, steadying him.

"I'm okay," Dick muttered. "I'm all right."

He stepped out of the stall, all eyes on him.

"So your tic . . ." the cadet with the glasses began.

". . . is that typos have the same effect on me that alcohol does," Dick finished. "You sweet kid, you."

Anna came out of the stall with Dick's target in hand.

"As you can see," she said, holding it up, "tics can be managed."

There were six shots in the dead center of the target's head. Dick nodded at his marksmanship, and promptly passed out.

He woke up some time later on the bed in one of the holding cells on the top floor of the Typo Squad building. He had no idea how much time had passed, but the window above his head looked out at the moon hovering in the night sky.

"Hey there," Thea said from the bed across the cell from him. He saw her fold over the corner of a page in a book and sit up from a reclining position. "How you feeling?"

"Fine." Dick swung his feet down from the bed to the floor. "One benefit of my tic is that I don't suffer hangovers."

Pain suddenly exploded in his head and he groaned out loud, falling sideways back on the bed. He held up a finger. "Okay, that was a lie. I didn't *used* to suffer hangovers."

"When you were . . . younger?" she asked with a teasing grin.

"Shut up, you." Dick massaged his temples.

"Well, hangovers aside, as tics go, yours isn't too bad."

"No, I suppose not," he said, moving his fingers from his temples to his forehead.

"That kid, the cadet who pisses himself when he sees a typo. Now that's rough."

"Too true," Thea said.

She gave him a little time for the effects of his typo hangover to pass. When he was finally sitting upright and his color was back, she spoke.

"Well, your first official day back on the force is over. We've got a rental car waiting in the parking garage for you, and you'll be staying at the department's condo until you get settled. Unless you prefer commuting to and from your cabin in Parts Unknown."

"No, the condo will do just fine," Dick said, rising. "Although I'll probably need blackout curtains to sleep."

He took a few steps toward the open cell door when Thea said, "What happened in Chicago?"

He turned to her. "Excuse me?"

"Chicago," Thea repeated. "You kept muttering it in your sleep."

"Oh." Dick shrugged. "I don't know why that would be."

"So nothing happened in Chicago?" Thea

pressed.

"No," Dick said. "I've never even been to Chicago."

"Then I wonder why you'd be talking about it in your sleep."

"Maybe I was thinking about the musical," Dick said. "It's got some really catchy numbers."

Thea stood. She looked ready to pursue the topic, but then her expression softened. "You know, one of the first things partners need is a sense of trust."

"Oh, are you my partner now?" Dick asked, raising an eyebrow.

"Yes. Tanka made the decision while you were dreaming about Chicago."

"Well, then." Dick extended his hand. "Sorry you drew the short straw."

Thea shook his hand firmly. "On the contrary," she said. "I think there's an awful lot I can learn from you. Starting with what happened in Chicago."

Dick used their clasped hands to pull her in close, and she gasped.

"I admire your determination," he said

softly. "But let this go. For now." He released her hand and added, "Please."

She nodded. "All right. For now."

"Thanks," Dick said. "Partner."

She smiled. "Hey, we're all going down to Merriam's for a drink tonight. Why don't you join us?"

"Merriam's?" Dick asked, surprised. "That old dive? We always used to get drinks down at The Galley."

"Yes, I'm well aware of Typo Squad traditions," Thea said patiently. "You'll be happy to know that we still go to The Galley, but it's closed on Saturdays now. The owner became a Seventh Day Adventist or something."

"Ah." Dick thought for a few moments. "Is Shwiski going to be there?"

Thea shrugged. "He's part of the team."

"Ugh," Dick said. "I hate that guy. But yeah, okay. I'll see you guys there."

CHAPTER FOUR

When Dick arrived at Merriam's bar, he found that Big, Thea, Anna, Ewan, Scott, and Tanka had already secured a corner booth near the back. The place was dim and looked to be on the verge of becoming a full-fledged dive. There were the dried corpses of long-dead flies on the unused pool tables in the middle of the room, and a dusty glowing jukebox played some old favorites in the background.

Dick sat down next to Anna. "Evening, all."

Everyone at the table greeted him, except for Scott, who stared fixedly at a glowing sign for one of the local beers. After a few moments, a waitress came to the table. She was short and very blonde, with a torn

AC/DC T-shirt that revealed most of her enormous breasts.

"Ho-ly Moses!" Big exclaimed. "Would you lookit the size of those—"

Anna elbowed him hard in the ribs.

"—earrings," he finished breathlessly.

"Funny," the waitress said, smiling. "Most often people comment on the size of my tits. What can I get everyone?"

"Rum and Coke," Tanka said.

"Make that two," said Anna.

"Tawny port," said Ewan.

"*Too-ney poot*," Big mimicked. "That's not a drink, that's a porn star's name."

"So is Big, I imagine." Ewan smiled.

"For you, sweetheart?" the waitress asked Dick.

He waved her off. "I'm good, thanks."

"Hon?" she asked Scott.

"Water," Scott said simply.

"And you?" she asked Big.

"Your finest Kentucky bourbon, my dear," Big said, cracking his knuckles dramatically. "And you might as well leave the bottle."

The waitress nodded. "And for you?" she

asked Thea.

"Chardonnay," Thea replied.

"Do you have ID, hon?" the waitress asked. There were grins all around the table and Dick stared at Thea for a moment. She did look incredibly young, though Dick noticed how much prettier she looked dressed in civilian clothing, with her red hair out of its tight ponytail.

Thea handed over her wallet and the waitress examined it. Her eyes got a bit wider and she smiled, looking back at Thea.

"Whoa. You're a member of Typo Squad?"

Thea nodded. "That's right."

The waitress looked around the table. "Are you all Typo Squad?"

"Yes . . ." Dick replied hesitantly, looking around at the others.

The waitress turned and called across the room to the chubby bald man behind the bar. "Joe! Hey Joe! C'mere!"

The man finished wiping down the bar with a grayish rag and ambled over. He had an open, cherubic face and a welcoming smile.

"What's goin' on?" Joe asked the waitress amiably.

"These folks," the waitress said, apparently bursting with the news, "are Typo Squad."

"No," Joe said, wide-eyed. "Are you really?"

"We are," Dick said, still hesitant.

"Well then your money's no good here," Joe said excitedly. "You guys do a hell of a job, I tell you. Hell of a job."

Everyone at the table exchanged glances.

"So . . . you believe that typos exist, then?" Dick said.

"Oh, I know they do," Joe said, stepping up to the table and leaning forward on his elbows. "My wife's cousin, Lanny. He was never right in the head. If you gave Lanny a ladder, you'd have to write 'stop' on the top rung."

Everyone laughed except Scott.

"Ol' Lanny never learned to read or write worth a damn," he continued, "but then one day he got it in his head to try and impress his folks by making them an anniversary card. He used crayons. Mind you, he was about thirty-five at the time. They say he misspelled 'happy.' Never even got out of the gate, did he? Of course Lanny couldn't read, so it didn't harm him none. But then he gave the card to his folks and they both dropped dead on the spot. Drove poor Lanny 'round the bend, and they had to put him away."

"I've been part of Typo Squad for most of my adult life," Dick said, "and that may be the saddest goddamn story I've ever heard."

"Yeah." Joe shrugged. "Well."

"Where did Lanny end up?" Dick asked. "Did they put him in Fula Ord?"

Joe cocked his head. "You know Fula Ord?"

Dick didn't reply immediately. He looked as though his thoughts had momentarily drifted elsewhere. But then he refocused and nodded. "Oh yeah. Lovely place. The paper slippers there hardly ever rip. Even if you're chewing your own toenails."

Joe chuckled. "Yeah, that's Fula Ord all right."

Dick extended his hand and Joe, surprised, shook it.

"Glad to meet someone who believes," Dick said. "Most people treat us like we belong in Fula Ord. And that typos are right up there with Sasquatch and the Loch Ness Monster."

Joe snorted. "Look, you just keep doing what you're doing and keeping us all safe, okay?"

"Will do," Dick said.

Joe left and headed back to the bar. The waitress lingered for a few moments, staring at Dick with a knowing smile. After she left to get the drinks, Big looked at Dick with a lascivious grin. "Oooh, I think she likes you," he sang.

"Seems like most of them do," Thea said with a wry grin.

"Same old Dick," Anna said. "How is it being back?"

"Weird," Dick said. "But in a good way."

"Maybe you should go back to the mountain," Scott said sourly. "If it's, y'know, too weird for you." Once again, he was roundly ignored.

"Not quite like the old days, is it?" Ewan

offered.

"All of your days are old days," Big said quickly.

"Christopher, isn't there a moon upon which you should be exerting a gravitational pull?" Ewan replied, unruffled.

"Hah!" Big barked. "That was a good one. I'll give you that one, gramps."

"I'm eternally grateful," Ewan said patiently. He turned back to Dick. "As I was saying, not quite the same as when you were taking down those errorist cells, eh?"

Thea suddenly leaned forward. "Oh, I wish I could have been part of Typo Squad in those days," she said wistfully.

"Those days are not as glamorous as they sound," Tanka said. "We lost a lot of good people. Though not nearly as many as we would have if not for Dick."

"My hero," muttered Scott, loud enough for the whole table to hear.

Tanka opened his mouth to say something, but at that moment the waitress returned with a tray of drinks, including a shot glass and a bottle of bourbon that she placed in front of

Big. He grabbed the bottle and admired it.

"Oh, I like this place," he said. "I like this place a lot." He poured himself a shot and hoisted it to eye level. "Gentlemen, ladies, if I may? To Typo Squad. *Lapsus calami.*"

Tanka stared at him for a moment, and then uncharacteristically grinned. He raised his own glass. "*Lapsus calami.*"

The rest of the crew raised their glasses as well, even Scott, while Dick unbuttoned his shirt pocket and pulled out the handful of dirty, beaten-up index cards. Under the table's overhead light, it was clear how yellowed with age they were and how many times they had been taped back together. He raised them and touched them to everyone's glasses as they clinked together. "*Lapsus calami.*"

He laid the cards out on the table. Written on them in black marker were various typos: MAINTENENCE. SIEZED. WITHDRAWL. Dick studied them and a drunken, easy grin spread across his face.

"Have I mentioned recently how much I envy his tic?" Big asked Tanka as he threw back his drink and poured another.

"Do you carry those with you while you're on duty?" Thea asked, a note of concern in her voice.

"They're strictly medicinal," Dick said easily.

"You could at least update the cards," Tanka said. "Those things are filthy."

"They've always done the job," Dick said lazily.

"You could copy the same typos onto new cards, is my point," Tanka said patiently. "I don't know why I bother sometimes."

"I don't know why you bother at all," Dick said.

"Can't you just have a drink like a normal person?" Tanka said.

"I suppose I could if I *were* a normal person," Dick said. "But let's face it."

"Yeah, true enough," Tanka said.

Everyone sipped their drinks.

"Feeling better, are you Dick?" Tanka said.

"Feelin' fine," Dick said, with an emphatic nod.

"Well, I'm glad to hear it," Tanka said. "Because I've got some news for you."

"Lay it on me, boss."

Tanka pointed at Thea. "This little firecracker is your new partner."

"Yeah, I know," Dick said. "She told me."

"Oh," Tanka said. "Then never mind."

Dick looked sideways at Thea. "Not that I really *want* to train a partner."

"Hey!" Thea said indignantly, giving Dick a shove for good measure. "For your information, I don't *need* training."

Dick blinked a few times and tried to focus. "Have you ever had a partner before?"

"Well," Thea said. "No."

"Then you need to be trained," Dick said. "It's a whole different thing."

"It's not so bad," Big interjected, throwing back a shot of bourbon. "I had to train a partner a couple of years ago. Oh man, you should have seen her. She looked like the business end of a bulldog."

"She and Big were practically twins," Ewan said quietly, taking a sip of his drink.

"And furthermore," Tanka said, with a long and meaningful look at Scott, "I'm reinstating you as field commander."

"Hey!" Anna cried. "Congratulations!"

Everyone looked delighted and hoisted their glasses, but Scott slammed his glass down on the table so hard it cracked. "*What?*" he cried.

"You heard me, Shwiski."

"That's *bullshit!*" Scott shouted, standing up and gripping the edge of the table. "You can't do that! I busted my ass to make field commander! And you just hand it to him on a silver platter because, what, he's *famous?*"

"Shwiski," Tanka said calmly, though Dick could see a familiar pink hue creeping out of his collar. "Do I have to remind you you're addressing a superior officer?"

"But he's—"

"The new Typo Squad field commander, so you'd better start getting used to it," Tanka cut in, his voice rising. The few other people in the bar were looking over with interest.

Scott's eyes bulged and he turned a deep shade of red as he looked from one team member's face to another, as if hoping someone would jump in and make a case for him. Everyone looked uncomfortably at their drinks.

"Fine," he said bitterly, looking down. "Fine, then. Lieutenant Tanka, consider this my resignation."

"Have it your way." Tanka shrugged.

Scott looked up one last time as if still seeking a sympathetic face, but everyone continued to look away. Without another word, Scott grabbed his jacket and stormed out.

An awkward silence followed until Big finally said, "Hey look at that! Something else to celebrate!" He hoisted his glass again, and everyone happily followed suit.

Dick watched as Scott yanked the front door of the bar open and slammed it just as hard closed. "You really made that asshole field commander?" he asked Tanka.

"I always choose assholes for field commanders," Tanka said, leaning his glass toward Dick. "Congratulations."

With their new friend Joe honoring his word that their drinks were on the house, the team ordered round after round of increasingly expensive liquor. Except for Dick, who kept pace by referring to his cards every now and then.

Eventually everyone at the table lapsed into a drunken silence, listening to the jukebox and the undercurrent of conversation. Dick leaned his face on his hand, his elbow propped on the table. Big was throwing back shots of bourbon with machine-gun regularity. No one was feeling any pain.

"So," Thea said suddenly, "you guys all worked with Dick for quite a while, right?"

There were nods all around.

"Since Dick is disinclined to do so, maybe one of you could tell me about Chicago."

The table fell into sudden, shocked silence. Everyone stared at Thea, and even Big had nothing to say. The moment spun out interminably, things growing more and more uncomfortable.

"Young lady . . ." Tanka said sternly, but Dick cut drunkenly across him.

"Chicago isn't a place," Dick said, and then chuckled. "Well, I mean, obviously it's a place, but the Chicago in my life is a person. Chicago Manuel. My stepbrother."

All eyes were on Dick.

"Y'see," Dick continued, his eyes half-lidded, "my parents divorced when I was a kid, and my mother married Chicago's father. Chicago and I were almost the same age—I was a year older—and we became as close as any two real brothers. We went to school together."

Dick smiled wide at the memory.

"When I was in fifth grade, they came around to do the testing to see who had the potential for Typo Squad. I was chosen. The following year, when he was in fifth grade, Chicago was chosen as well. Isn't that something? He and I didn't share genes, but as it turned out, we were both chosen."

Dick's expression darkened. "Chicago's dad, my stepfather, didn't want Chicago to go to the academy. He didn't care what I did, since he and I never really got along, so I jumped at the chance. Chicago didn't know what to do. He was scared. He wanted to know what I thought he should do. I was selfish. I convinced him to join me at the academy. We both graduated with top honors."

Dick paused to stare at his index cards for a moment. No one at the table said a word.

"He was my first partner. I loved working with him. He used to make fun of me because of my tic. Chicago was one of those one-in-a-million agents who didn't have a tic. Typos didn't affect him in any way. At least, that's what we all *thought*."

"Dick," Anna said gently, reaching across the table and taking his hand. "Don't."

"It's okay," Dick said. "It's all right. You know, it's actually nice to be talking about Chicago. I get a lot of the credit for busting up the errorist cells, but he was right there with me. He deserves the recognition."

Thea swallowed hard. "So what happened to Chicago?"

"Like I said, he was that rare bird with no visible tic, but it turns out the typos were affecting him after all. It's just that none of us knew it. The typos were slowly driving him insane."

No one said a word. No one even breathed. The silence was palpable.

"By the time we figured it out, it was too late," Dick said thoughtfully. "He was lost. There was no getting him back. I had no choice but to commit him to Fula Ord. He's been there for the past five years."

"Is that . . . is that why you left?" Thea asked.

"Yeah," Dick said. "I couldn't handle it. I couldn't face him. It was my fault. He never wanted this life. I talked him into it."

"Dear boy, there's no way you could've known," Ewan said gently. "And I remember so clearly how much it meant to him, being your partner. He may have gotten the short end of the proverbial stick, but he was doing what he loved with the brother he loved. Surely that counts for something."

Dick nodded. "It does. Thanks, Ewan."

"I've known heartache of my own," Ewan said. "Have I ever told the story of my time in Buckingham Palace?"

"Yes," everyone said together. Ewan looked from one face to another, and suddenly the table was filled with laughter.

The festivities carried on until after midnight, when only the waitress, the bartender, and Typo Squad remained.

"Whelp," Dick said at last, stepping out of the booth and steadying himself on the table. He gathered up his index cards and tucked them into his breast pocket. "This was fun."

"Hear hear!" Big roared, finishing off the last of the bourbon. He closed one eye and used the other to look into the empty bottle. "Anyshing leff?"

"Well's dry, buddy," Dick said. "Time to go."

Tanka raised his head off the table and looked around. Ewan had dozed off and was snoring softly, his head pitched to the side and resting on his shoulder. His silver hair gleamed in the overhead light.

Thea's eyes were half-lidded and a little smile held to her lips as she propped her head up with her hand. Anna's eyes were closed and she sang softly and out of tune along with the song playing on the jukebox.

"Yeah, it's probably time to . . . we were . . . to be getting. Home," Big said, moving sideways out of the booth. He slid right off the end and into a heap on the floor.

"Mmm?" said Ewan, stirring at the sound of the crash. He looked blearily at Big's prone body and nodded. "Mmm."

Tanka and Dick, both still unsteady themselves, got themselves under each of Big's arms and hoisted him up. The others stood and joined them.

"I think you should cab me a call," Big said with a wide, lopsided grin.

"Yeah, I'll cab a call for all of us," Dick said, helping Tanka guide Big toward the door as if they were in a three-legged race. Joe the bartender raised a hand in a cheery wave. They passed the waitress at the end of the bar on their way out.

"Oh, I wouldn't want to leave without saying goodbye to those!" Big bellowed, and the waitress smiled broadly.

"Thanks for the hospitality," Dick said.

"Anytime," she replied.

The unwieldy trio led the others out the

bar's front door. Their shadows crossed the Merriam's sign on the window and disappeared.

CHAPTER FIVE

After three days in the city, Dick still couldn't sleep.

The department's condo was clean, spacious, and comfortable. But it was also bordered downtown, where the ambient noise of the city and the glow of the streetlights on the edges of the bedroom curtains kept sleep entirely at bay.

He checked the bedside table clock. It was just past one in the morning. He was so tired he felt it deep in his bones, but he swung his legs out of bed and passed a hand through his hair. Maybe a little exercise would help.

So he found himself dressed and wandering the deserted streets of Los Palabras in the still of the very early morning. He wandered through the downtown area, a part of town that used to be lined with factories that belched their filth into the air, but had been converted to trendy spots that fed and watered the disposable income crowd.

He passed a faded stop sign. He was about to turn the corner when something caught his eye: the darkness of a storefront was broken by a flashlight beam dancing around the inside walls and windows.

He sighed, legitimately torn. He could just call it in and let the regular cops handle it. The odds that whatever was happening required a Typo Squad agent were practically nil. Still . . .

Dick turned back and trotted over to the outside wall, away from the orange circle of light from a nearby street lamp and out of sight of whoever was inside.

He took a few steps forward, hugging the smooth brick wall, then stopped and considered for a moment. He took a step back, dug into his pocket, and pulled out his phone. His thumb scrolled past a litany of names until he fell upon TANKA. He pressed the call button and waited.

"What? What? What is it? What do you want?" an angry, groggy voice said after multiple rings.

"Oh, nothing," Dick whispered, keeping an eye on the storefront. "Just wondered what you were dreaming about. Why do you *think* I'm calling?"

"Oh, Jesus. Please don't tell me you're handling something that LPPD could handle. Please don't tell me that."

"Well, I won't know until I've started handling it, will I?" Dick said. "The place on the corner of Fifth and Briggs. Do you know it?"

"Fifth and Briggs," Tanka repeated. "Yeah. Yeah, I know the place. It's an organic café. It's called, uh . . . Whey Cool, I think."

Dick pulled up short. "You know an organic café?"

"I know a lot of things, smartass," Tanka snarled.

"Do you know why someone would be fumbling around in Whey Cool with only a flashlight?"

"No, and I don't care," Tanka said. "You

know why I don't care? Because that's a B&E, Dick. And we don't handle B&Es. The regular police do. So call the regular police and let me go back to bed, willya?"

"I can't be sure it's a B&E until I go in and have a look."

"Oh my God," Tanka said. "You're gonna make me have to come down there. Aren't you?"

"Only if you want to."

"If I get out of this bed," Tanka said menacingly, "and I get dressed, and call the rest of the Squad, and drive all the way down there, and it turns out to be some kid rifling through the cash register for pot money—"

"Okay, great, see you soon," Dick interrupted, and hung up quickly. He stuffed the phone back in his pocket, unholstered his sidearm, and crouched his way under the front window of Whey Cool and around to the front door.

Keeping as low to the ground as his aging knees allowed, he crept silently in and hid behind a booth. The shadows cast the café in crisscrossing shades of gray. He peered around the edge of the seat and assessed the situation.

It was a heavyset girl, her brown hair pulled back in a loose ponytail under a Whey Cool visor. The strings holding her apron around the back strained to stay tied. In her left hand she held a flashlight, and in her right was a dry erase marker, busily updating the specials board for the next day.

Dick cursed himself. There was nothing illegal going on; it was just some teenage kid trying to get a jump on her work. As he contemplated a variety of scenarios to make a discreet exit and not scare the shit out of the poor girl, he watched her finish up by writing the day of the week at the top of the board.

But instead of writing THURSDAY, she wrote THRUSDAY.

Dick felt it immediately. The cafe suddenly pitched sideways and blurred. The familiar warm euphoria spread throughout his body. He began to giggle, suppressing it on the back of his hand.

With a drunken half-grin on his face, he stood suddenly and swayed. He raised the gun and pointed it straight at the girl.

"Freeze!" he shouted in the silence, and his voice rang off the walls. The girl screamed at the top of her lungs, threw the marker and flashlight away, and put her hands in the air as high as they could go.

"Don't kill me!" she howled and immediately began to cry. Dick did his best to focus on what was happening, but the room wouldn't stay level and the girl kept doubling and blurring.

"It wasn't my idea!" she babbled. "He said I could make some extra money! He said it was just a joke and no big deal!"

Dick could hear sirens off in the distance. He only needed to hold on for a little while longer and then someone else could take his place so he could pass out properly.

"Who's he?" Dick asked.

"The man in the mask!" the girl cried. "The man in the mask!"

Dick heard tires screeching to a halt outside, and the café was suddenly flooded with alternating blue and red lights.

"Siddown," Dick slurred, and gestured

with his gun to the booth nearest the girl. She continued to weep hysterically, keeping her hands high in the air. Dick took a few unsteady steps toward her, and then something important occurred to him. He dug out his cell phone and once again called Sergeant Tanka.

"Dick?" the voice said through the speaker.

"Tanka," Dick said, and then chuckled to himself. "You out there, you beautiful pile of crab rangoon?"

"What's the situation?" Tanka asked.

"Damn kid put up a damn typo," Dick slurred. "Gimme a second to lock it down."

"We're standing by," Tanka replied.

Dick staggered over to the dry erase board and, keeping his eyes downcast, grabbed a nearby rag and erased the whole thing.

"All clear," Dick said, and heard the rush of footsteps and shouting as he calmly passed out.

Dick felt a cold, hard bench under his back, and heard himself groan softly as he came around. He opened his eyes tentatively, and saw a giant ass hovering just inches away from his nose.

"Goddammit, Big," he growled, and punched the right cheek as hard as he was able.

"Ow!" Big cried. He moved away, rubbing his wounded backside. "Just for that, next time I'll fart."

"And here I thought that farting was your primary form of communication," Dick heard Ewan say.

"Hey, that reminds me, I've been meaning to ask you," Big said. "Weren't you one of the waiters at the Last Supper?"

"Shut up, the both of you." Dick grunted, slowly moving to a sitting position. He let out a low groan and put his hands on the sides of his throbbing head.

"Oh, don't be so dramatic, will you?" he heard Tanka say. "You'd think that typo nearly killed you."

"I wish it'd killed *you*," Dick said. He looked around. The café lights were on. Surrounding Dick was the rest of Typo Squad.

The teenage girl was seated nearby, handcuffed and looking sullen and defiant.

"So?" Tanka prompted. "Are you gonna fill us in on what happened here?"

Dick pointed toward the girl. "That sweet young thing over there was writing up the specials menu," he said. "She intentionally misspelled Thursday."

"Jesus Christ." Anna hooked her thumbs into her uniform belt. "Do you know how many people might've died if you hadn't caught her?"

"Yep, I'm a hero, all right," Dick said, rubbing his forehead. He turned to Tanka. "Do heroes make more money?"

"You'll get a raise when I'm long dead and complaining to the devil that hell's not hot enough," Tanka replied.

"Sweet," Dick said. "Two things to look forward to."

"Are you gonna talk to her?" Tanka said.

Dick nodded, stood slowly, and then paused. "Hold on a second." He gestured that Tanka, Ewan, Big, Thea, and Anna should move in closer. Dick lowered his voice.

"She said that someone told her the typo was a joke, a way for her to make some extra money," Dick said. "And that it was a man in a mask."

They all exchanged glances. Tanka rolled his eyes. "Oh, just what we need," he sighed. "A masked lunatic running around, bribing young girls to make typos."

"Hey," Big said suddenly. "How come she's not dead?"

Everyone turned to look at him.

"What?" he said defensively. "You said she misspelled Thursday. How come she's not dead then?"

"He's got a point, boss," Anna said. "She might be one of us and not even know it."

"We'll sort that out later," Tanka said. "Dick, see what she knows."

Dick looked at Tanka. "You wanna play good Typo Squad agent, bad Typo Squad agent?"

Tanka grabbed him by his vest and steered him toward the girl. "Just get talking, will you? I was having a beautiful dream when you rang, and I'd like to get back to it."

Dick approached the girl's table and sat across from her. "Hi there," he said, extending his hand. He leaned to the side and looked at her handcuffs. "Oh, right. Sorry."

"I didn't do anything wrong!" the girl spat.

"What's your name?"

"Bite me," the girl said with a snarl.

"Huh," Dick said. "Is that German?"

The girl looked away. "Elizabeth," she said sullenly.

Dick leaned back in his chair, crossing his ankles and putting his hands behind his head. "You know, you're in a shit-ton of trouble, Elizabeth." The girl turned back to him. "Oh yeah. We can book you on attempted murder. Suspicion of errorism. Animal cruelty."

The girl looked up. "Animal cruelty?"

Dick pointed at Ewan. "You see that silver fox over there? Because of you, he had to get out of bed and come all the way down here. I'd call that cruel."

"Though, to be fair," Ewan piped up, raising a finger, "I *was* already awake for my late-night ablutions."

"Ew," Big said. "I really hope I die before

I get old."

"Yes," Ewan said. "I hope that as well."

"So," Dick continued. "Should we head down to the station? We might be able to find you a cell with smallish rats. Big cockroaches, though."

"But I didn't do anything *wrong*!" the girl whined, and her cocksure attitude vanished. She was just a scared girl again.

"You answer some questions for me and maybe we can work something out, " Dick said.

"Questions about what?"

"The man in the mask." Dick leaned forward.

"What about him?"

"How did you two cross paths?"

"I don't know," the girl said. "He just showed up after we closed tonight. He tapped on the window, wanted to come in."

"And you let him? A guy wearing a mask?" Dick asked.

"Hey, have you *seen* some of the people in this town?"

"Fair enough," Dick said. "Describe him."

"He was tall. Kinda thin. He had on a black suit, black shirt, black tie. And the mask."

"What did the mask look like?"

"I think it was leather," the girl said. "There were holes for his eyes and mouth, but that's it. Oh, and the asterisk."

"Asterisk?" Dick said.

"Yeah. It was silver, right in the middle of his forehead. Like a badge, almost."

"A silver asterisk badge in the middle of his forehead." Dick looked over his shoulder at Tanka, who shook his head.

"Hey, you asked," the girl said. "Okay, I described the guy. Can you let me go now?"

"Not so fast," Dick said. "Tell me about your conversation with him."

The girl's expression suddenly softened. "He was really nice. Really charming. Told me he thought I was pretty."

"Oh, Jesus Christ," Tanka muttered in the background.

"He asked me if I'd be in on a joke that he wanted to set up," she continued. "He gave me a hundred dollar bill and just told me to misspell 'Thursday' on the specials board. He said there was plenty more where that hundred came from, and if all went well, I could come work for him."

"Work for him where?" asked Dick.

"I don't know," she said. "We never got that far. And since things didn't exactly go well, I guess I'll never know now."

Dick mulled over what she'd said, then rose from his seat. "Sit tight." He crossed the room to where the rest of his team stood.

"Well?" he said.

"I think she and the masked man will make an adorable couple," Big said, making a heart shape in the air with his fingers.

"Big, you're aware how many people could have been killed by that typo, right?" Thea said.

"Yeah," Big replied. "Zero. Because big Dick was on the scene."

"I could actually live with being called big Dick," said Dick.

"Lieutenant?" Ewan said, cutting across the conversation. "Thoughts?"

"If everything she said is true," Tanka said,

"then we've got a guy who could potentially be bribing impressionable young kids all over the city to put typos up."

"Which means we need to find him fast," Anna said.

"Shouldn't be too extreme of a challenge," Ewan said. "A gentleman in an all-black suit with a leather mask bearing a silver asterisk tends to stand out."

"All right," Tanka said. "Everyone go home and get some rest, will you? We'll start on this case first thing in the morning."

"What, we don't get to sleep in after all this?" Big said.

"Fine, sleep in! We'll start it first thing after lunch!" Tanka growled. "Why do you constantly have to bust my balls, Big?"

"You have to play to your strengths, boss," Big said innocently.

Dick jerked his head toward the still-handcuffed girl. "What about her?"

"Let her go," Tanka said. "But keep her information handy, will you? If the typo didn't kill her, there are better things for her to be doing than making kale smoothies."

Dick nodded. He crossed over to the girl and sat down again.

"Okay," Dick said. "We're gonna let you go. But first I need you to do something for me. I need you to raise your right hand."

The girl moved her hands to the side to indicate the handcuffs.

"Oh. Right," Dick said. "Okay then, just repeat after me: 'I solemnly swear that I will never intentionally misspell a word again as long as I live.'"

The girl sighed. "Really?"

"Do you want to wrap this up or not?"

"*Fine,*" she hissed. "I solemnly swear that I will never intentionally misspell a word again as long as I live."

"Good," Dick said. "See that you don't."

He circled around her and unlocked the handcuffs. She rolled her shoulders a few times and massaged her wrists.

"Here's my contact information," Dick said, handing her a card. "If you remember anything else about the man in the mask, you call me, okay?"

Dick joined his team as they began

shuffling toward the door when the girl said suddenly, "Don't you even want to know the guy's name?"

Everyone stopped in their tracks and turned back to her.

"He told you his *name*?" Dick said incredulously.

"Yeah," the girl said. "His name is Anton. Anton Nym."

CHAPTER SIX

The next day, Dick crowded with Thea, Big, Ewan, and Anna around a wobbly table in a tiny conference room. An ancient whiteboard with the ghosts of words that would never totally come off sat in a corner, under ceiling tiles that were browning with water damage.

Tanka came into the room and closed the door behind him. Under his arm was a beat-up old laptop. He looked dour.

"Well, Dick," he said without preamble, setting up the laptop so that the screen faced the others, "it seems you've got a fan."

He pressed the play button on an open video. Black-and-white static filled the screen for a moment, and then a figure replaced it. It was a man in a black suit wearing a leather mask with a silver asterisk in the middle of his forehead.

"Hello, Richard," Nym said in a gravelly, digitally distorted voice, and all eyes turned toward Dick. "My name is Anton Nym. And I have a proposition I wish to present for your consideration."

Nym ran a gloved hand over the top of his mask and took a deep breath.

"Return to the mountain. And no one need suffer." He stared for a long time at the camera, as though awaiting a response from Dick.

"I'm only here because you are," Nym continued. "Do you understand?"

Dick stared at the computer blankly.

Nym leaned forward, his whole face filling the screen. "If you return from whence you came, I will do so as well. But if you remain here with Typo Squad, I'll have no other recourse than to unleash hell upon the citizens of Los Palabras."

Nym leaned back in his chair and put his hands casually on top of his head. "It's entirely in your hands, Richard. I leave it to you," Nym said. "Knowing your penchant for playing the hero, I can imagine that you are not afraid of me. You're probably already thinking that you'll find me and slide the noose on me. It's your duty to bring villains like me to justice, after all, and you will."

Nym leaned forward again. "No you won't, Richard. No you won't. If you remain, I'm going to thin out your fan club, a million people at a time. You can't stop me. I know you'll feel compelled to try. But I shall drown this city in typos. I shall drown this country in typos. And just as God did in Noah's time . . . I shall drown the *world*."

Nym stood up, walking out of the shot, but his voice called out from beyond the frame: "*Lapsus calami!*" Dick felt goosebumps rise on his forearms.

The screen cut back to the black-and-white static before fading to black. The conference room was silent.

"Well," Dick said at last. "At least he's well spoken."

"Yep," Big said. "Snappy dresser, too."

"He may be threatening innocent civilians,

and we certainly must make every effort to find and apprehend him," Ewan said, "but I must say, it's a bit of a thrill to have a legitimate villain again. We haven't had one of those since that fellow a few years back, the one with the pregnancy pun for a name. What was it again?"

"Mister Period!" Big cried out.

"Yes, that's the one!" Ewan said, delighted.

They looked to Tanka, who was stone-faced. "Oh no, don't let me interrupt," Tanka said. "Please, keep making jokes while a lunatic is on the loose."

"Sorry boss," said Big.

"My apologies, Lieutenant," Ewan added.

Tanka turned to Dick. "Do we need to discuss Nym's ultimatum? Are you considering going back to the mountain?"

"Run away?" Dick asked incredulously. "From that bondage-mask-wearing nut job? I thought you knew me better than that."

"I'm glad that I do," Tanka replied. "Any idea how this guy might know you?"

Dick shook his head. "No."

"Well, then," Thea said. "It looks like we need a plan."

"We already have a plan," Tanka snapped. "We've got every cop in the city looking for this wacko. In the meantime—"

He was cut off when a frantic officer slammed the door open. "Lieutenant! They need the team down at Strunk Field right away."

"Why?"

The officer shook his head. "I dunno. Some guy named Nym called in, said he's gonna try something."

Tanka looked from the officer to his team. "Why are you all sitting there? Move!" and everyone scrambled to their feet.

The SUV carrying the team squealed into the parking lot of Strunk Field with siren wailing and lights whirling. The side door was open before they'd even come to a full stop and Dick, Thea, Big, Ewan, and Anna piled out and headed straight for the main gates.

A group of regular cops was milling around near the entrance, looking calm and relaxed. Dick approached them. "What's the situation?" he asked the nearest officer.

"Well I'll be damned," the cop said. He was tall, with graying temples and a deeply lined, tanned face. His teeth were dazzling against his bronze skin.

"Why will you be damned?" Dick asked.

"Because Shonnary has finally come out of retirement," the cop said excitedly, and before he had time to react, Dick was pulled into a tight bear hug.

"Okay," Dick squeaked, his lungs suddenly empty. The cop let go and pulled off his cap. The graying temples gave way to a perfectly smooth, bald head. The cop smiled and offered Dick his profile.

"Oh, for Christ's sake." Dick laughed in spite of himself. "Cody. How are you doing? Goddamn, I didn't even recognize you."

"Yeah, well, it's been a while," Cody said, offering his hand, which Dick shook. "Where the hell have you been all this time?"

"Oh, you know, hiding out in the woods," Dick replied. "Like you do."

Cody's smile faltered. "Well. Nobody can

blame you for that. I imagine you had a lot to think about."

"Yeah," Dick said. "Yeah, I did."

"So, anyway, what brings Typo Squad down here?" Cody returned to his businesslike demeanor. "Tanka spring for tickets to the game?"

Big barked out a laugh. "Oh, that'll be the day."

Anna stepped forward. "We were told there was a situation down here."

Cody looked at his fellow officers, who merely shrugged. "If there is, we haven't heard about it."

Dick turned to the rest of his team. "What do you think?"

"Wouldn't hurt to have a look around," Big said. "Grab a hot dog, a couple of beers. Maybe some Cracker Jacks."

"Can you focus for me?" Dick said. "Please?"

"What? I am focused," Big said innocently. "Just on different things than you are."

"Come on," Dick said to the team.

"Good seeing you, Dick," Cody called

after him. "Give me a call. I'll buy you a drink."

They passed under the sign that read WELCOME TO STRUNK FIELD! HOME OF THE LOS PALABRAS SEMICOLONS, and below that, PROUD AAA AFFILIATE OF THE LOS PALABRAS COLONS. They moved onto the concourse, then down a long concrete tunnel as the bright green of the field slowly revealed itself.

Everything looked perfectly normal. The stands were filled with fans dressed in purple, the home color of the Semicolons, and the low buzz of conversation was cut by a few whistles, shouts of encouragement directed at the players, and vendors hawking their wares.

The team lined up on the walkway between the lower and upper sections.

"See anything?" Dick asked, surveying the field.

"Yeah." Thea pointed up at the scoreboard. "We're getting our asses kicked."

Dick looked up. The scoreboard over right field showed SEMICOLONS 2, ELLIPSES

13.

"Oof," Dick said. "That's . . ." his voice trailed off as he saw the animated screen at the top of the board flicker for a moment, and the message WELCOME FANS! suddenly became WELLCOME FANS!

He looked away just in time; a wave of dizziness hit him, but not as hard as it might have.

"Dick?" Ewan said, and he heard the concern in the old man's voice. "What is it? What's wrong?"

"Scoreboard," Dick managed, his eyes tight shut, and a few seconds later he heard a cacophony of sounds: Ewan giggling helplessly, Anna being violently ill, Big shouting "Nut sacks!" and Thea making odd gasping noises. He made a quick mental note to ask her what her tic was, but at the moment there were more pressing issues.

Dick opened his eyes and grabbed Thea, who was closest to him, pulling her up out of a crouch.

"Find a fire alarm and pull it," Dick instructed. She stood up straight, took a deep breath, and vanished down the tunnel they'd come through.

"Ewan," Dick said, and Ewan covered his mouth to hold in the giggles he was wracked with. "Find someone who can cut the power." Ewan nodded, his eyes spilling over with hysterical tears, and he disappeared as well.

Dick turned to Big and Anna, who was wiping vomit from her chin with the back of her glove.

"We've got to keep these people from looking up at the scoreboard," Dick said. "Any ideas?"

Anna and Big looked at one another, and Big said firmly, "Yeah, I've got this."

Before Dick or Anna could say another word, Big yanked off his vest and pulled his uniform shirt over his head. His giant belly quivered.

"Uh," Dick said, but that was all he had time for. Big bounded down the nearest flight of stairs, vaulted the barrier, and ran out onto the field.

The low hum of the crowd grew louder as people spotted him. Soon they were pointing and standing, whistling and hollering as Big made his way to the middle of the outfield. He stopped right in front of the Semicolons' center fielder, put his hands on his hips, and began to gyrate in what could only charitably be called a dance. The crowd didn't seem to care, and their egging him on only drove him to more complex and crazed movements.

Dick watched transfixed as Big's body swayed and shimmied, ripples dancing up and down his belly. He heard Anna retch and puke hard next to him.

"I told you not to look at the scoreboard," Dick said.

"I didn't." Anna spat the last of it from her mouth.

Security guards in bright yellow polo shirts had joined Big on the field, but Big was deceptively quick and agile for a big man. As they tried to restrain him, he made a break for the infield. The players, who had stopped the game when Big arrived, now backed away and headed to the relative safety of their respective dugouts.

Just as Big reached home plate, the power

in the stadium cut out and everything went dark. A few seconds later, a fire alarm began to whoop and a recorded voice came over the PA, saying, "Ladies and gentlemen, please make your way to the emergency exits in a calm and orderly fashion. Thank you."

The statement continued on a loop as the people in the stands began shuffling toward the exits. Thea and Ewan rejoined Dick and Anna.

"Mission accomplished," Thea said with a small salute. She glanced down at the field. "Oh dear God."

The security officers had a hold of the shirtless Big and were frog-marching him off the grass.

"Hey," Dick called, moving down to the field to meet them. He produced his Typo Squad badge and ID. "He's with us. Believe it or not, he was saving lives."

"With my sick dance moves," Big added.

The security officers released Big. Anna handed him his shirt and uniform gear, and he dressed.

The stadium had nearly emptied and Dick

and the rest of the team stood on the dirt near the Semicolons' dugout, keeping an eye on the stands. Dick couldn't suppress a smile.

"This is actually pretty cool," he confided to the others. "Standing down here on the field? I feel like a kid again."

"I suppose, if you're a fan of baseball," Ewan said. "Now if you want a real sport, you truly can't beat football."

"You mean soccer?" Big asked.

"I mean football," Ewan replied.

"English football," Big clarified.

"Yes, English football." Ewan sounded nettled.

"So soccer," Big said with a mischievous grin.

"Big," Ewan said, drawing a deep breath, "your mother—"

He was interrupted by a loud bray of static from the scoreboard, which had inexplicably come back to life. The rest of the power in the stadium remained off.

The impossibly large face of Anton Nym filled the screen.

"You," he said, his digitally altered voice

booming and echoing. "You ruined my day at the ball game."

He moved in closer to the camera. The light source at his end accented the grain of his leather mask, and the silver asterisk at his forehead glinted evilly. "I see you've made your decision, Richard," he said. "I shall enjoy forcing you to jump through hoops for my amusement. You'll be hearing from me."

The scoreboard went dark once again. No one said a word for a few moments.

"You were saying about my mother?" said Big.

The next day, Dick arrived at headquarters to a flurry of activity. Nym's attempt at attacking a large crowd seemed to have lit a fire under everyone, and the buzz of conversation and the sound of ringing phones were louder than usual.

The team gathered around Dick's desk, but before anyone even had a chance to wish each other good morning, Tanka approached. He held a folder in his hand, which he slapped down on the desktop.

"Nothing!" he exclaimed. "Not a goddamn thing. The forensics team swept Whey Cool and the stadium, and didn't come up with so much as a single fiber or fingerprint. They ran facial recognition software on the video and came up empty."

"They ran facial recognition on a mask?" Big asked earnestly.

"There are things you can learn," Tanka snapped.

"Are you sure?" Dick asked. "If they didn't find anything?"

"Shut your holes, the both of you," Tanka growled. "I talked to the mayor this morning. Catching Anton Nym is now our number-one priority."

Tanka turned to Anna. "I want you to start profiling all the former errorists we have in the database. See if one of them might be Nym."

"You got it, boss," Anna said, and headed off.

"You two," Tanka said to Big and Ewan. "Seeing as she's the only one who's ever met him, find that girl from Whey Cool, get her in here, see if she remembers anything else about Nym."

"Jolly good," Ewan said, and he and Big left.

"And you two," Tanka said to Dick and Thea. "Head over to the Grammatica. See if they know anything about this guy."

"The what?" Thea asked blankly.

"You'll see," said Dick. "C'mon, I'll drive."

CHAPTER SEVEN

Twenty minutes later, Dick and Thea pulled up in front of a huge, austere-looking building. With its brick facade, white columns, and wide front steps that ran the entire length of the portico, it could have been any of a dozen government buildings. The only thing missing was some sort of sign or indicator of what purpose the building served, of which there were none.

"This is it?" Thea asked, as they both got out of the SUV.

"It is," Dick said.

"What's inside?"

"The Grammatica houses all the CLITs in Los Palabras."

Clear excitement crossed Thea's face. "Are

you serious?"

"Yep."

"Wow," she said as they moved toward the first set of steps. Before they'd even made three stairs, a voice called out to them.

"Yo, Richard!"

They both turned and spotted a young man standing in a small grassy area adjacent to the Grammatica. He was short and skinny, with a prominent nose and beard that looked like it couldn't decide whether or not to grow. He was dressed in a hoodie that was two sizes too big, baggy jeans, and work boots.

Thea followed behind as Dick approached the young man with his hand extended and a smile on his face. As they shook hands, the young man smiled as well.

"Well I'll be damned," Dick said. "How are you, Subscript?"

"Workin' it, you know," the young man said. "S'all good. Ain't seen you in a dog's age, Richard."

"You know I prefer Dick."

"Yeah, I read that on a bathroom wall somewhere," Subscript said, and laughed. "By the way, it ain't Subscript no more. It's Superscript."

"Ah," Dick said. "Moving up in the world?"

"Aw, man," Superscript said, rolling his eyes. "Couldn't resist, could you?"

"I'll just go ahead and introduce myself," Thea said, extending her hand. "Thea Saurus."

"What's up?" Superscript said, shaking her hand as well. He turned to Dick. "New partner?"

"Yep," Dick said.

"Does she know what happened with all your old partners?"

"Even I don't know what happened with all my old partners," Dick said.

"So," Thea said, "how do you two know each other?"

"Subscript—" Dick began, but stopped himself. "My apologies, old habits. Superscript here used to be the bane of my existence. He was the leader of a bunch of troublemakers called the Blueline Gang. They ran wild all over Los Palabras, spray painting typos on any surface they could find."

Superscript chuckled, looking down at his shoes. "Yeah, too true. Too true. Got in a shitload of trouble. But ol' Dick here saved our asses."

"Oh?" asked Thea. "How so?"

"Well, intentional posting of a typo is a felony," Superscript explained. "So we were all looking at some serious prison time. But Dick talked to the judge on our behalf. Said he could set us straight."

"And, with no false modesty, I did," Dick said to Thea.

"He did," Superscript said. "Put us on community service, repainting everything we defaced. Taught us responsibility."

"And if I'm doing the math right, and I'm probably not, you and the rest of the Blueliners should be eligible in a few months," Dick said.

"That's right," Superscript said. "The first of September."

"Eligible for what?" Thea asked.

"The judge said if we could keep our noses clean, he'd clear our records and we could apply to Typo Academy," Superscript said.

"It's gonna be close, but I think we'll just make the cutoff for the fall semester."

Dick put a hand on the young man's shoulder. "I'm proud of you."

"Yeah, well," Superscript said, turning slightly pink. "Don't make it all weird."

"All right," said Dick. "I'll resist the urge to hold you and stroke your hair and tell you what a good boy you are."

Superscript turned to Thea. "I think he was all alone on that mountain for too long."

"You don't know the half of it," Thea said.

"What are you doing here anyway?" Dick asked suddenly.

"Oh, we're repainting the side of the Grammatica," Superscript said. "Look."

He pointed to scaffolding lining the outer wall of the building. Two figures dressed similarly to Superscript were hard at work with paintbrushes and rollers.

"Hey, Brackets!" Dick called, waving. "Hey, Carat!"

The two figures stopped what they were doing and waved back enthusiastically.

"Hey!" one of them called back. "We'll be

Typo Squad before you know it! Save us the best lockers!"

"I have the best locker!" Dick called back. "But I'll see what I can do!"

They resumed their painting and Dick turned back to Superscript. "All right, Thea and I have work to do. Stay out of trouble, okay?"

"Will do," Superscript said. "Good seeing you."

Dick moved to head inside, but then turned back.

"Hey," he said. "The name Anton Nym doesn't ring any bells, does it?"

Superscript shook his head. "No. Should it?"

"New player in town," Dick said. "Keep your ears open for me, would you?"

"Anton Nym," Superscript repeated. "Okay, I'll let you know if I hear anything."

"Good man." Dick headed back toward the building steps, Thea close behind. Together they climbed the dozen or so short flights to the front doors, which were carved of ornate oak and had oversized brass pulls mounted on plates. Dick paused, looking at Thea, whose face was filled with excitement and anticipation.

"Brace yourself," Dick said. "This place can be a little overwhelming."

They went inside.

The doors opened into a large marble antechamber. A pair of guards stationed on either side of a gilded archway checked their credentials and waved them through.

The antechamber gave way to a cavernous room beyond. Massive crystal chandeliers hung from the cathedral ceilings. The walls and railings were done in highly polished mahogany. Thick burgundy carpeting covered the floors, cushioning their footfalls.

Dick and Thea were on the second floor, which was open to the area below. As Thea approached the balustrade overlooking the first floor, Dick heard her gasp.

The floor below them had walls lined with bookcases that were stuffed to capacity with books of every size and shape. Dotting the floor were beautiful European-style desks, and seated at those desks were men and women sitting in the most comfortable-looking chairs, all of them wrapped in fluffy robes, all of them reviewing papers with red pens in hand. Circulating around them were men and women dressed in all black with pristine white aprons, taking drink orders, offering massages, and in some cases, performing pedicures. Soft chamber music played from hidden speakers.

"What . . . what is this?" Thea asked breathlessly.

"Those folks wrapped up in the fuzzy robes," Dick said in a quiet voice, "are CLITs."

"This is the life that CLITs lead?"

"It is."

"What the *hell*?" Thea said. "Why did I join Typo Squad, then?"

"Shhh!" Dick hissed. "Keep your voice down!"

"Fine!" Thea hissed back. "Why did I join Typo Squad then?"

Dick looked down over the unquestionable pampering going on below.

"Eh, I imagine all that luxury and being waited on hand and foot gets old after a while." They watched one of the men in black deliver a glass of champagne on a silver tray with a proper bow to a robed figure.

"And the CLITs' only job is to review public-facing documentation and make sure it's clean?" Thea asked.

"That's all," Dick said.

"God *damn*." Thea didn't take her eyes off the splendor of the first floor. "Is it too late for me to choose a different career path?"

"*Richard*!" a voice suddenly cried. Dick and Thea both turned to see a dark-haired woman in a smart suit approaching them quickly. The woman threw her arms around Dick's neck and kissed him hard on the lips.

"Unbelievable," Thea muttered as the woman let go of Dick and took a step back, smoothing her hair and her clothes, her eyes locked on his face and a huge smile on hers.

"Hey Lauren," Dick said. "You know I prefer Dick."

"Oh," the woman said breathlessly, "oh yes, so do I."

Dick smiled. "It's been a long time."

"Too long!" Lauren playfully punched Dick on the arm. She turned to Thea. "I know quite a few CLITs that will be thrilled to see Dick."

Thea's eyes widened and she blinked twice, slowly.

"This is my new partner, Thea Saurus," Dick said. "Thea, this is Lauren Ipsum, executive director of the Grammatica."

"How do you do?" Lauren said, shaking Thea's hand enthusiastically. "New partner, wow. You certainly must see a lot of Dick."

Thea blinked again. "Um," she said, but Lauren was already focused again on Dick.

"So what can I do for you?" she asked. "Is this a social visit, or business?"

"Business," Dick said, and Lauren's smile faded just a bit.

"Pity," she said. "Still, you're here, and that's what's important." She turned to Thea. "I get ever so excited when Dick is in here. You know?"

"Um," Thea said once again.

Lauren hooked Dick's arm. "Come on, we

can talk in my office."

Lauren's office was at the far end of the building, and had an expansive window behind her desk overlooking the CLITs' level down below. Dick and Thea settled into the guest chairs and Lauren leaned forward on her elbows, fingers intertwined.

"So," she said, smiling. "How can I help you?"

"It seems I have a new nemesis," Dick said. "We were wondering if you might've heard anything about him."

"Ooooh, that's exciting," Lauren said. "Nothing like a villain to keep you on your toes. What do you know about him?"

"He calls himself Anton Nym," Thea offered. "He dresses all in black and wears a black mask with a silver asterisk in the middle of the forehead."

"Well," Lauren said thoughtfully, "at least he's got style."

"Does any of that ring any bells?" Dick asked.

Lauren shook her head. "No, sorry, it

doesn't." Then sudden alarm grew on her face. "You don't think this Nym character has any errorist ties, do you?"

"Can't rule anything out right now," Dick replied. "I certainly hope not."

"Oh, those were dark times, Dick," Lauren said with a small shudder. "Dark times."

"Why, what happened?" Thea asked.

Lauren turned to her. "Oh yes, you're probably too young to remember. There were errorist cells everywhere. Everywhere. They were trying to sneak typos through any way they could. My people were working night and day, running their red pens dry trying to keep up.

"And of course, the tics!" she continued. "Well, you'll know all about tics, I'm sure. They're manageable if you only find a typo every now and then. But that first floor sounded like a lunatic asylum in those days."

She stopped herself, and then looked pleadingly at Dick. "Oh, I'm so sorry, Dick. Please forgive me; I wasn't thinking."

Dick shrugged it off. "No worries."

"Well, anyway," Lauren said, picking up

the thread of her story, "Dick was able to rid us of the errorist threat, and things went back to normal around here. And to thank the CLITs for all their hard work, the mayor started a fund to make sure that they were comfortable and well looked-after. You may have noticed they enjoy a bit of luxury."

"Yes, I did," Thea said. "In fact, if you have any application forms handy, I'm definitely interested in handing in my Typo Squad badge and trying life as a CLIT on for size."

Before Lauren could answer, they heard a loud *bang!* from somewhere outside the office.

"What on earth was that?" Lauren asked, mystified.

Bang! Bang! The sound seemed to be getting louder, and now was blended with screams and cries.

The trio rushed to the window that overlooked the first floor. Standing there at the opposite end of the space, his black clothes a stark contrast to the tranquil white of the floor, was Anton Nym, a massive, smoking silver pistol gripped in his right hand.

Several of the CLITs were dead, their heads nearly blown off from the caliber of the bullets, their white robes stained with shockingly bright red blood. The other CLITs and servants were running in every direction for cover.

"Call for help!" Dick shouted over his shoulder, sprinting for the office door, Thea hot on his heels. He ran out onto the gallery and stopped at the railing that overlooked the lower level. He unholstered his weapon and aimed it at Nym. Thea followed suit.

"Freeze!" he screamed, and Anton's masked head snapped up. Before Dick or Thea could react, Nym fled out the front entrance.

Dick and Thea sprinted down the gallery and through the entranceway. The two guards who had checked them in now lay in pools of blood on the marble floor.

When the two agents reached the entrance, they shouldered into the doors at full speed, but they were jammed shut.

They stepped back and began to throw forceful kicks at the doors, both of them putting all their weight behind the blows, and they slowly began to give. On the last kick, the doors flew open and Dick and Thea nearly spilled out onto the topmost step. They hurtled down the first flight of steps when Dick suddenly threw out an arm and stopped Thea cold.

She followed his gaze down the stairs. Standing in the middle of the street was Nym, his arm wrapped tightly around a struggling Superscript's neck. His weapon was pointed straight at Superscript's temple. People on both sidewalks were screaming and running for cover.

"Were I you," Nym called to them, his voice still low and distorted, "I would divest myself of any and all weaponry."

Dick and Thea exchanged a quick glance, and then as one, lowered their guns down to the stair on which they stood, dropping their weapons.

"Now I should ask that you create a distance of separation between yourselves and said weaponry," Nym said. He was maddeningly calm, even though Superscript kept squirming and trying to get his hands in between his throat and Nym's forearm.

Dick and Thea each kicked their guns off to the side, raising their hands halfway up. "Don't hurt the kid," Dick called to Nym. "This is between us."

"Fundamentally, yes, it is between us," Nym said. "But as I stated very clearly in my earlier missives, as you have decided to remain here, I intend to cause you the most harm by bringing harm to the innocent. I know full well how painful and maddening it will be for you to watch them suffer."

"No!" Dick shouted. "Please."

On squealing tires, a limousine appeared from a side street and barreled toward Nym. It stopped, its passenger side door directly behind him. The window rolled down and the door flew open from within.

"Young man," Nym said calmly to Superscript, "I am, generally speaking, not one to try and offer any sage advice, but in this instance I shall make an exception. Do not follow Richard into a path that leads inevitably toward Typo Squad. It'll only end in pain and misery."

Nym locked eyes with Dick for a moment, then turned back to his prisoner.

"I shall now release you and step into my awaiting vehicle," Nym said, and at these words, Superscript ceased struggling. "But I warn you not to move in any way, to try and harm me or escape, or I shall end your life in a very messy way. Are we agreed?"

Superscript nodded as much as he was able, and Nym slowly released him. Nym's gun was still trained directly on him, and the young man stood rooted to the spot in the middle of the street, his hands now up, his quivering legs threatening to collapse him into a heap.

Nym stepped backward, sat down in the limo's rear seat, and closed the door, keeping his weapon trained on Superscript through the open window.

"I implore you to walk away from this, Richard," Nym called out. "Return to the safety of your mountain retreat. If you remain part of Typo Squad, there will be naught but tragedy."

Nym pulled the trigger. The report echoed off the steel-and-glass buildings and into the evening air. Superscript pitched forward and fell to his knees, a crimson bloom spreading on the front of his sweatshirt, a look of disbelieving shock etched on his young face.

The limousine took off as Nym rolled up his window, disappearing down the nearest side street. Dick and Thea both dove for their guns, but by the time they had them in hand, the limo was long gone.

Dick vaulted the stairs two at a time, Thea directly behind him. He dove for the prone figure in the street and jammed his fingers into the side of Superscript's neck. Nothing. He looked helplessly at Thea, who put her hand up to her mouth, tears welling in her eyes.

CHAPTER EIGHT

Dick paced restlessly around the condo that night, passing by the index cards laid out on the kitchen counter. He read them over and over again, but no matter how much they triggered his tic, he couldn't escape the image of Superscript lying dead in the street, covered in blood, his once-bright future snuffed out in an instant.

Without even realizing what he was doing, Dick grabbed his suitcase, opening it on the couch in the living room. He began throwing his few possessions in it.

There was a knock at the door.

"Leave me alone."

"It's Tanka," the muffled voice said from the other side.

"I don't care if it's a three-headed leprechaun here to bring me a fucking pot of gold," Dick called. "Leave me alone!"

The lock made a soft clicking sound and the door swung open.

"Of course," Dick said. "Of course you'd have a key."

Tanka took in the scene. "Going somewhere?"

"Of course I am," Dick replied. "Didn't you hear what happened today?"

"Dick," Tanka said, his voice low, "he was a good kid. Okay, maybe not a good kid, but he was a kid who was really trying to turn his life around."

"Yeah, and because I didn't listen to Nym's warning, that kid is dead," Dick said, his hackles rising. "So I'm going back to the mountain like I should've done in the first place."

"Huh." Tanka moved over to the suitcase, slamming the lid shut. "So you're one hundred percent sure that if you go away, he'll go away?"

"If he doesn't, the rest of you can handle

it," Dick said, stepping right up to Tanka and opening the suitcase again. Tanka slammed it shut once more.

"Same old Dick." Tanka's voice was low with barely controlled anger. "Running away when things get tough."

Dick's fury ignited like a flare. "You didn't hold a dead kid's head in your hands today!" he shouted, now almost nose-to-nose with Tanka. "A kid who was dead because of me!"

"Superscript isn't the only one who died!" Tanka screamed back, and Dick stepped back as if slapped. "That son of a bitch also killed eight people in the Grammatica!"

"I . . ." Dick began, but trailed off. He stepped over to the kitchen counter and stared at his cards. "I forgot."

Dick tried to keep his mind blank, but Tanka's words had sunk in. In his focus on Superscript, he had completely forgotten about the guards and the CLITs who had died first. He sat down heavily on one of the living room chairs. Tanka sat on the end of the coffee table, facing him.

"Dick," he said, much more calmly now,

"you're the best I've got. You've always been the best. But I need to know I can count on you. I need to know you're going to be here. I need you to help stop this guy."

Dick thought it over. After a while, he nodded.

"Thanks," Tanka said. "Can we get to work?"

"Not right now." Dick pointed toward the nearby index cards.

Tanka nodded. "Okay, then." Tanka took off his coat. "You go lie down and sleep it off. There'll be fresh coffee when you wake up."

Dick grunted in agreement, headed to the bedroom, and fell headfirst into a black, dream-free sleep.

When he awoke, he was surprised to find himself in the passenger seat of Tanka's car, headed toward Typo Squad headquarters.

"The hell?" he said thickly, trying to bring the world into focus.

"Oh good, I won't have to carry you when we get there," Tanka said. "Once is enough. And I thought Big was unwieldy."

"Why'd you muscle me into the car?" Dick asked, rubbing his eyes.

"Because all of the important stuff is at headquarters," Tanka said. "So the sooner we get back to work, the better."

"Urgh," Dick said. "Hey, you promised me coffee."

Tanka reached down and grabbed a travel mug. "Cream and nine sugars. Just the way teenage girls like it."

Dick took the coffee and sipped it, blinking hard and trying not to watch the city speeding by outside.

"This is why I didn't want to come back, Tanka," Dick said suddenly. "I knew someone would get hurt."

"A lot more people are going to get hurt if you don't see this through," Tanka replied. "Look, I'm sorry, okay? I thought you needed to come back. I thought it would give you purpose again. I thought you needed a team again. Maybe I was wrong. But we've got this Nym mess to clean up right now. Once that's done, if you want to leave again and stay gone forever, I won't stop you."

Dick pressed his head against the cool glass of the passenger side window and closed his eyes. "Sometimes I really wish I were dead."

"If we're not careful," Tanka said, "you just might get that wish."

At Typo Squad headquarters, the mood was somber. Dick and Tanka passed through the lobby, Autumn stopping Dick to give him a long hug and offer her condolences. Inside, Big, Ewan, and Anna offered theirs as well.

"Where's Thea?" Dick asked. Anna pointed toward the locker room.

Dick opened the locker room door and heard soft sobbing. He peeked his head around and saw Thea sitting on the floor, knees up, head resting on her crossed arms. Her hair was down, and Dick noticed once again how lovely it was when it wasn't pulled back into a tight ponytail.

He crossed the room and sat down beside her.

"The first time I saw somebody killed in the field," Dick said softly, "I went straight home. Didn't finish out my shift, didn't clock out, didn't tell anyone where I was going. Just went home. I didn't know what else to do. I remember going into the kitchen, grabbing a bowl and some cereal and milk, without really knowing what I was doing. And when I went to pour the cereal, it spilled all over the kitchen table because my hand was shaking so badly."

Thea raised her head, sniffed, and wiped tears away from her cheeks. Her eyes and face were almost the same shade of pink.

"Yeah?" she said, her voice watery. "Then what?"

"Then I scooped up all the spilled cereal and dropped it back in the box. I stood up, walked calmly to the bathroom, and puked until I burst a blood vessel in my eye."

Thea chuckled a bit.

"Listen," he said, putting an arm around her shoulder and pulling her close, "it's all right to feel what you're feeling. Okay? It's normal. It means you're human and that you haven't become jaded. But as my partner, I'm asking you to put all of what you're feeling aside for now. We have a murdering shit-bag out there that we need to catch. And we need to make him sorry he ever laid a finger on Superscript or those guards or any of those CLITs. Can you do that?"

Thea sniffed again, looking up at Dick. "Yeah. Yeah, I can do that."

The moment spun out. Dick gazed deeply into Thea's green eyes. Dick noticed his pulse had quickened. Even red-faced and puffy-eyed, Thea was truly beautiful.

He leaned forward a bit. So did she.

"Are you guys gonna kiss?" came Big's voice from behind a set of nearby lockers.

Dick saw Big's head peering around the corner, a wide, knowing grin across his face. He only hovered there for a moment before Anna's gloved hand reached in, hooked his ear, and yanked him away.

"Ow!" Big protested as he was led out of the locker room. "Hey! Quit it! C'mon, they were gonna kiss!"

"That's nobody's business but theirs," Anna said. "Out!"

Dick looked back at Thea, who looked

marginally more cheerful.

"Come on," she said. "Let's get to work."

They exited the locker room to find a chaotic scene. Tanka was standing at the far end of the room behind a podium that bore the Typo Squad logo on the front. Gathered around him were dozens of men and women in suits, all holding notepads and recorders, and various cameramen. Big, Ewan, and Anna stood off to the side and toward the back, away from the commotion.

As Dick and Thea joined ranks with their teammates, Big nodded at the scene.

"Press conference," he whispered. "This should be great. Tanka's *really* bad at press conferences."

"I don't remember him being really bad at press conferences," Dick said.

Ewan leaned forward. "He hasn't the patience he had five years ago," he said. "And five years ago, he hadn't much patience to begin with."

"Good evening, ladies and gentlemen," Tanka began. He was already sweating, and his face was pinker than usual. "I'm here to confirm that at 4:53 this evening, in and around the Grammatica building on Twelfth Avenue in Los Palabras, a perpetrator was involved in the murder of nine individuals."

There was an immediate ripple through the reporters and many of them stood, shouting questions.

"I'm not finished, goddammit!" Tanka snarled, and the reporters all sat down as if slapped.

"The perpetrator goes by the name Anton Nym," Tanka continued. "He is known to Typo Squad, though this is the first instance that we know of where he's resorted to firearms instead of typos. A description of Nym will be distributed shortly. He should be considered armed and extremely dangerous, and citizens of Los Palabras are urged to contact us with any information they might have. Now I'll take questions."

Dick leaned over to Big. "I thought you said he was really bad at these."

Big smiled. "Give it a minute."

The group of reporters rose once again,

and a confused babble broke out. Tanka pointed to a young woman in the front row, and the rest quieted to let her talk.

"Lieutenant Tanka," the reporter said, "do you know of any motives behind the killings?"

"What a stupid question," Tanka said. "What am I, a goddamned mind reader? How the hell do I know why this nut-job is killing people? Next question."

An older reporter jumped up. "Lieutenant, will you be releasing the names of the victims?"

"What kind of a ghoul are you?" Tanka retorted. "Are you planning to dance on their graves, too? No, we're not releasing any names. Next question."

Another woman stood. "Lieutenant, does it appear at this time that Anton Nym might have errorist ties or leanings?"

"Listen to yourself," Tanka said disgustedly. "There are no more errorists. Jesus, do your research. Next question."

A younger man stood and raised his pen in Tanka's direction. "Lieutenant, will you be coordinating efforts with any of the other typo divisions?"

"What, you think my team can't handle this on their own?" Tanka barked. "For your information, we've recently brought Dick Shonnary back into the fold, so I think we're more than prepared."

He gestured to where Dick stood with the rest of the team. All heads swiveled toward Dick, and in one wave, the reporters abandoned Tanka and made their way over to him, shouting questions and snapping photos.

"Something I said?" Tanka asked.

The next morning, Dick arrived for work and found Thea waiting for him at his desk.

"Before you get comfortable, c'mon," she said heavily.

"Where are we going?"

"To see the quartermaster." Thea was already heading toward the stairwell that led to the police station next door.

"What for?" Dick asked, following her.

"We need to get you fitted for your dress uniform."

"Dress uniform?" Dick said with clear

distaste. "Why do I need a dress uniform?"

Thea stopped and turned back to face him. "Superscript's funeral," she said simply.

The sun shone down brightly as Dick and Thea arrived at Gramadach Cemetery. His dress uniform was as uncomfortable as he remembered, but when he spotted Ewan, Big, Anna, and Tanka gathered at the gravesite in their finest, he had to admit they looked impressive. Their dress jackets, pants, shoes, and hats were all similar to the Marines' dress, except Typo Squad's were all black with a red belt and the agency's insignia on the shoulder and the front of the cap. They lined up with the rest of the team, and Dick looked around. The turnout was depressingly small; beyond Superscript's former gang member friends, Brackets and Carat, there were a handful of mourners.

As they waited for the priest to arrive, Dick whispered to Thea, "Who paid for all this? Superscript didn't have any money."

"Tanka did," Thea whispered back.

Dick leaned forward slightly to see the

lieutenant's face. It was stoic and unreadable, but in that moment, Dick felt a great swell of affection toward him.

After the funeral service, and once again dressed in their tactical uniforms, the team gathered in the small, shabby conference room. Anna sat across from Dick and Thea with an open laptop, and Tanka sat at the head of the table.

"Okay, let's get a solid description of this asshole in the system," Tanka said. "How tall would you say he was?"

"About six foot, maybe six one," Dick answered. Anna typed the information in.

"Weight?"

"Between one-eighty and two hundred," Thea said. "Thin build, but strong."

"Did either of you get a look at his skin tone?" Tanka asked.

Dick and Thea looked at one another, and both shook their heads.

"He was covered head to toe," Dick said. "The black mask with the silver asterisk, and then a black button-down, black tie, black suit jacket, black dress pants, and black shoes and socks. Oh, and black gloves."

"Right-handed or left?" Tanka asked.

"He had the gun in his right," Thea answered.

"And what kind of gun?"

"Nickel-plated Hardballer Longslide," Dick replied.

"Anything distinctive about his voice?"

"He was using the same type of voice changer that he used in the video," Dick said. "No idea what he really sounds like."

"Did he say anything that might give us an idea where he'll turn up next?"

Once again, Dick and Thea looked at one another, and once again they both shook their heads.

"Sorry, boss," Thea said.

"At least we've got something to go on now," Tanka said. "Anna, upload that info to the database and make sure everyone has access, will you?"

"I'm on it," Anna said, typing away.

"Lieutenant," Ewan said quietly. "Don't you feel that we have an obvious suspect in all of this?"

Tanka gave him a confused look.

"No," Tanka replied. "Do you feel that we do?"

The room went quiet, all eyes on Ewan.

"I do," Ewan replied.

Tanka sat down at the head of the table. "Then by all means, let's hear it."

"Agent Shwiski," Ewan said simply.

"Scott?" Anna asked. "No, that's crazy."

"Have any of you seen him since he quit?" Ewan asked.

Everyone looked at one another. No one had.

"He appears to fit the physical description," Ewan continued, "and he certainly has a gripe against Dick."

Anna shook her head. "No," she repeated. "Scott's an asshole, but he's not a killer."

"He seemed quite incensed when he stormed out of Merriam's," Ewan said. "Angry people do terrible things."

Tanka stared at the table, deep in thought. "Boss?" Dick asked at last.

"It's not enough to bring him in for

questioning," Tanka said, "but let's see if he's willing to come in on his own. You know where he lives?" he asked Anna. She nodded.

"Go and talk to him," Tanka said.

"And be sure to give him our best," Big said sweetly.

"Dick," Tanka said.

"Oh, I know that tone," Dick groaned. "You've got an idea, and I'm not going to like it."

"I've got an idea," Tanka sighed, "and you're not going to like it."

"Great. What is it?"

"It might be time to talk to Penny," Tanka said, without looking at Dick.

"Ah, shit," Dick said.

"Who's Penny?" Thea asked.

"Red Penny. A former Typo Squad agent," Tanka said. "She lives on the street now, and she can be a really solid source of information."

"Well, that's great!" Thea said. "Why wouldn't you want to talk to her?"

Dick shifted uncomfortably in his chair.

"Oh, for Christ's sake," Thea said,

exasperated. "Not her, too."

Dick merely shrugged.

"It's actually a bit more complicated than a simple dalliance," Ewan chimed in. "Red Penny at one time filled the same role you now do. She was Dick's partner."

"Oh," Thea said. "I see."

"Is talking to Penny a request or an order?" Dick asked Tanka.

"She might be our best bet to find out who Nym is," Tanka said. "So you tell me."

Dick thought it over for a moment, then nodded. He stood up, turning to Thea. "Come on," he said. "Let's go see what Penny knows."

CHAPTER NINE

Dick and Thea drove across town in silence, pulling up in front of the Los Palabras Art Museum just after sundown. A ground fog crept along the sidewalks, casting the streetlights in a ghostly haze.

"She should be down there," Dick said as they got out of the car. He pointed to a narrow alleyway that ran between the museum and the customs house next door. They made their way to the darkened mouth of the alley, and together they navigated the tight quarters of trash cans, dumpsters, and bloated rats scurrying in and out of hiding places.

The alley ended in a chain link fence, and a makeshift shelter made of a refrigerator box and an assortment of appliance blankets stood propped against it. Dick grabbed a small flashlight from his belt, pulled aside the tatters, and peered in.

"Penny?" he called, but there was no one there.

"Now what?" Thea asked. Dick looked around. On the other side of the fence, a homeless man, all stained clothing and missing teeth, slept against the wall with a nearly empty bottle cradled gently in his arms.

"Hey!" Dick called. "Hey!"

The homeless man stirred and looked up at Dick with watery, bloodshot eyes. Dick presented his Typo Squad badge.

"You know Red Penny?" Dick asked.

The man nodded.

"Where can I find her?"

With great effort, the man lifted his ragged fingerless glove and pointed up and behind them. Dick turned and saw a gleaming multistory building across the street. He turned back.

"What? She lives over there now?"

The man nodded and then fell back into a fitful doze.

"Come on," Dick said, and he and Thea threaded their way out of the alley.

The building across the street couldn't have been more than a few years old, and boasted a beautiful wood-paneled lobby with a concierge. Dick and Thea approached the man, a thin balding fellow with a graying mustache and reading glasses balanced on the end of his sloped nose.

"Evening, folks. How can I help you?" he said.

"I'm Agent Shonnary; this is Agent Saurus," Dick said, presenting his badge. "Typo Squad."

"Agents," the concierge said, nodding. "What can I do for you?"

"We're looking for a woman called Red Penny. We were told she lives here now, although I can't imagine that's true."

"Oh yes, I know her. She moved in last month. She took one of the penthouse apartments."

"What?" Dick asked. "How is that possible?"

"I'm not sure what you mean, Agent Shonnary."

"Well, unless her fortunes have changed dramatically, the Red Penny I know is homeless."

The concierge shook his head. "Then we can't be talking about the same person. The woman I know is well-appointed and, if you'll forgive me, appears to have money to spare."

Dick pondered this for a moment. "The penthouse, you said?"

"Yes sir. Twenty-first floor, unit 2109. Elevator's around the corner to your left."

"Thanks."

Dick and Thea made their way to the elevator. "What are you thinking?" Thea whispered.

"I'm not sure what to think just yet."

The elevator arrived and they stepped on. Dick took the opportunity to dip into his pocket and pull out his index cards. He glanced at them quickly, and then tucked them back where they'd come from. Thea eyed him beadily but said nothing.

It was a quick, smooth ride to 21, and the

door to Penny's place was directly in front of them when the door opened.

Dick stepped forward and knocked.

The door swung open and a glamourous woman with coppery red hair stood in the entryway. She wore a long green silk dress and matching heels, which accentuated her hair and the spray of freckles across her nose perfectly. In her left hand she held a martini glass. The easy, drunken smile on her face faded when she saw who was in the hallway.

"Oh," she said, deflated. "It's you. Hello, Richard."

"I prefer Dick."

"Live and let live, I say," Penny said with a shrug. She eyed Thea. "New partner?"

"Yeah. This is Thea Saurus."

"Of course it is," Penny said, swaying slightly on her heels. "What do you want?"

"We want to ask you what you know about Anton Nym," Thea said baldly.

Penny's face betrayed nothing, but she didn't ask who Anton Nym was or immediately deny that she knew anything. She seemed to be debating what to do, and at last she stepped away from the door and muttered, "Fine. Come in."

The apartment was sumptuous: deep pile carpeting, an oak mantel over the fireplace, granite countertops, and a magnificent view of the twinkling lights of Los Palabras.

"Nice place, Penny," Dick said.

"You noticed." Penny toasted him with her glass.

"You, uh, win the lottery or something?"

"In a manner of speaking," Penny answered vaguely.

"You know, this Anton Nym character that we're looking for," Dick said, "he's partial to some pretty expensive suits. Seems like he's got money."

"Good for Anton Nym," Penny said. She drained her martini in one swallow and crossed the living room to the bar to begin fixing another.

"Last time I saw you," Dick pressed, "you were squatting under a bridge and didn't have two nickels to rub together. Now you're living large. How does that work?"

Penny turned, looking at him blearily.

"Oh, so *now* you care where I'm living?"

Dick immediately tensed up. Penny seemed to notice, and judging by her expression, it pleased her.

"Funny how you never worried about my financial situation when I was out there living like an animal."

"I tried to help you," Dick said. "You know I did. You just never let me."

"Tried to help me," Penny muttered. "Like you tried to help me when they drummed me out of Typo Squad?"

Thea's eyes widened. "What?"

"Oh, your new boyfriend didn't bother telling you that?" Penny said, smiling drunkenly.

"He's not my boyfriend," Thea said.

"I don't care if he's your tax accountant," Penny growled. "Did he tell you about he and I?"

"I know that you were once partners," Thea said uncomfortably. "In more ways than one."

"In more ways than one," Penny echoed, with a spiteful grin on her face. "Oh, I couldn't have put it better myself."

"Penny," Dick said.

"No," Penny continued, "by all means, let's fill in the details for your new partner. Maybe it will keep her from making the same mistakes I did."

A sudden silence filled the room, checked off by the faint ticking of a grandfather clock in the corner. Easy, drunken tears welling up in Penny's eyes. "Dick and I were really quite the team in those days," Penny said, and the tears began to flow, tracking mascara down her cheeks. "Weren't we, Dick? We were both young and fresh out of the academy. They normally team up the kids with more experienced Typo Squad agents, but somehow we ended up together."

Penny took a swig of her drink, stood up unsteadily, and weaved her way over to the couch where Dick sat. "We shared an office and a bed for years," she continued. "And then one day . . ."

It appeared as though Penny either couldn't or wouldn't continue.

"And then one day what?" Thea prodded.

"Dick and I and the rest of the team had just taken down an errorist cell," Penny said, not taking her eyes off Dick's face. "We were all out celebrating. I was watching Dick in his glory, drinking and laughing with the others. That was the moment I realized that I wasn't just attracted to him. That I wasn't just sleeping with him. That's when I knew I loved him."

"Penny, stop," Dick said.

"I told him that very night," Penny said, continuing on as though Dick hadn't spoken. "I waited for the perfect moment. We were walking home from the bar down a cobblestone street. It was late, there wasn't a soul to be seen anywhere. It was snowing. Softly. I slowed down under an old-fashioned streetlamp and pulled him close to me. And told him that I loved him."

In that moment, Penny seemed to be back on that very cobblestone street, and a wistful smile spread across her face.

"And what happened?" Thea asked quietly.

"He said . . . he told me he didn't feel the

same way," Penny said. "It sh-shattered me."

Dick looked at the floor. Penny wouldn't break her gaze away from his face. Thea watched them both, transfixed.

"I tried to make it work," Penny continued, sniffling. "I said that we could just go back to being partners. And we did. But it was making me crazy. I couldn't see straight. I couldn't do my job. I was biting people's heads off. Finally they gave me my walking papers. I was forced out of Typo Squad. And that was that."

"But then how did you end up homeless?" Thea asked.

Penny finally looked up at Thea, as if coming out of a trance. "Dick and Typo Squad were all I ever had. I didn't have anything left or anything to look forward to, so I became fast friends with the bottle. Everything spun out of control from that point. I wound up living on the street. And that's where I've been ever since."

"Until now," Dick said finally.

"Until now," Penny echoed. She toasted him and threw back the rest of her drink.

"Where did the money come from, Penny?" Dick said.

"Anyone ever tell you you've got a one-track mind?" Penny was beginning to slur now, and her eyes were unfocused. "Of course, when you and I shared a bed, that was a good thing." She cackled laughter and looked to Thea. "Am I right, sister?"

"The money," Dick persisted.

"Oh, for Christ's sake," Penny grumbled. "Fine! Nym gave me the money!"

Dick grabbed her suddenly by the shoulders. "Penny! Nym is a mass murderer!"

"That's where we are, Dick," Penny said, her voice dripping with disdain. "A mass murderer is more concerned about me than you are."

Dick pushed her back roughly on the couch, shaking his head. "Are you working for him?"

"No," Penny said patiently. "He pays for me to live here and gives me a nice life. I was a street person, Dick. Someone wants to pull me out of the gutter? Fine. I don't ask questions."

"Where can we find him?"

"That," Penny said flatly, "I couldn't tell you."

"Because you don't want to or because you don't know?"

"Yes and yes," Penny said, and promptly passed out. The martini glass hit the carpet with a dull thud and rolled under the sofa.

Thea turned to Dick. "Thoughts on how we should proceed?"

Dick looked at the snoozing Penny with a mixture of pity and distaste. "Well, she's of no use to us now."

"Should we come back when she's sober?"

"You saw how cooperative she was tonight when she was sober . . . well, more sober," Dick said.

"We could take her in, see if she'll be more cooperative in the holding tank," said Thea.

"Hold her for what?" Dick said. "Letting Nym buy her things?"

"Associating with a known felon should be enough," Thea said.

Dick thought it over, but shook his head. "We don't know she's associated with him since he became a felon," he said. "And it's nothing but a drunken confession. It's just too thin."

"Okay then," Thea said. "What do you suggest?"

"I suppose since we're here, and she's in no fit state to protest, it wouldn't hurt to have a look around," Dick said with a smile.

Thea smiled back. "And we really should keep an eye on her, make sure she doesn't choke on her own vomit."

"Too true. You can easily die that way."

"Okay, well," Thea said, moving toward the kitchen, "why don't I look around for a bucket in case she's sick, and why don't you check the bedroom to see if there's any aspirin. She may need it."

Dick nodded. Thea went to the kitchen while Dick moved into the master bedroom. It was as nicely appointed as the rest of the apartment. Every surface gleamed and not a thing was out of place, almost like a museum.

Dick rummaged through the bedside tables, but there was nothing of interest. When he opened the door to the walk-in closet, he spotted a large cardboard box tucked away behind a jumbled pile of shoes. The label on the side indicated it had arrived recently from a publishing company.

Dick dragged the box out to the middle of the bedroom floor and flipped the top open. Sitting in a pile of packing peanuts was a book. Dick pulled it out and brushed it off.

"The hell?" Dick said aloud. The title read THOUGHTFUL MEDITATIONS FOR A HECTIC LIFE and the author was listed as Su Do Nym.

"Thea!" Dick called. "Have a look at this."

Thea joined him and he handed her the book. "Su Do Nym," she read, chuckling. "Subtle."

She flipped to a random page and read, and almost immediately clenched her legs together and fell to her knees, gasping and moaning.

Dick snatched the book out of her hands and tossed it away, as though it were a poisonous snake come to life. He watched Thea writhing in pleasure on the floor, pulling herself into the fetal position, her breath coming fast and heavy as intense ecstasy seemed to course through her body. It became more and more uncomfortable, so he stepped out into the living room where Red Penny still sat, snoring softly with her head on her shoulder.

After about ten minutes of slowly decreasing paroxysms of joy, Thea emerged from the bedroom and joined him. Her face was flush and she pulled her ponytail back into place.

"Whew!" she said. "Those were some good typos."

"So," Dick said, awkwardly, "your tic . . ."

". . . is intense orgasms, yes," she finished brightly.

Dick nodded. "People have told me for decades how jealous they are of my tic," Dick told her. "I think those same people would say that same thing about yours."

Thea shrugged. "Good genes, I guess."

"So can I assume that *Thoughtful Meditations for a Hectic Life* hasn't been properly copyedited?"

"Oh no," Thea said. "That thing's a mess."

"Well then," Dick said, sitting down in a comfortable armchair and putting his feet up on the coffee table, "we'll have a lot to talk about when this one wakes up, won't we?"

Penny's deep, drunken slumber became a light and fitful doze. When she woke, she was surrounded by Lieutenant Tanka and the rest of Typo Squad.

"Oh God." She looked around at Tanka, Big, Ewan, and Anna. "It's like the worst high school reunion imaginable."

"It's nice to see you again too, Penny," Tanka said. "We have a few questions we'd like to ask you."

"I want a lawyer," Penny said, blinking heavily and folding her arms.

"You're gonna need one," Anna said.

"Oh, hey, Anna," Penny said with mock sincerity. "Still hanging around with the cool kids, I see."

Big turned to Ewan. "She called us the cool kids. She really must have tied one on."

"Indeed." Ewan nodded.

"So," Tanka said. "Read any good books

lately?"

Dick handed him the copy of *Thoughtful Meditations for a Hectic Life*, and he held it up for Penny's examination.

"Where did you get that?" she barked.

"It was just laying around," Dick said. "In a box. In your bedroom closet. Under some shoes. You really ought to be more careful about where you leave things."

"So this is Nym's next play," Tanka said, examining the book. "Publishing a book riddled with typos. If it hits the best-seller list, he could kill off half the country."

Penny stared at him, tight-lipped and defiant.

"What I don't understand," Dick jumped in, "is how he thought he was going to get away with this. Every book goes through the Grammatica. Surely he must've known it would never reach the public."

Penny snorted and shook her head.

"Yes?" Dick asked.

"You guys are so stupid."

"Hey!" Big said. "Easy now. I'm definitely stupid, but these guys aren't. Well, okay, he is," he finished, pointing to Ewan.

"Please, tell us why we're so stupid, Penny," Tanka said. "I'm anxious to hear this."

Penny sighed deeply, and then, with the patient cadence of a first grade teacher, said, "How many guns did Nym have on him when he killed all those CLITs at the Grammatica the other night?"

"One," Dick said. "So what?"

"And how many CLITs did he kill with it?"

"Six," Dick answered.

"He had plenty more bullets in the clip," Penny said. "Why stop with six? He could've killed a lot more, and a hell of a lot more if he'd brought a second gun, right? So why only six?"

Dick looked blankly at Tanka, who shrugged. He looked at the rest of the team, but no one seemed to have an answer.

"See?" Penny grinned. "Stupid."

Thea stood up, looking suddenly terrified. "Because the rest work for him," she said breathlessly.

Penny clapped her hands and laughed. "Ah, you hired a kid with a brain! Good for you!"

"He only killed the ones that he couldn't coerce," Thea gibbered, "but the rest will let any typos through that he wants them to."

"Oh my God," Dick said.

Tanka was on his phone in a flash. "Autumn, get a hold of the LPPD—have them send every available officer to the Grammatica. Tell them to put the place on lockdown until I get there, understood?"

"You can keep sticking your fingers in the dam," Penny said sagely, "but that bitch is still gonna burst."

"We'll see about that," Dick said. "Anything else you'd care to tell us? We're so stupid, after all."

"Nope," Penny said. "I'm done talking. Now be a good boy and fetch me another martini, would you? Stirred, please."

CHAPTER TEN

When Dick and Thea arrived back at Typo Squad headquarters later that night, Los Palabras cops were everywhere, booking and taking confessions from CLITs who looked hopelessly out of place in their fluffy white robes with their hands cuffed behind them. Dick sought out Tanka, who was being pulled in a dozen different directions.

"Penny was right," he blurted out as he ran past Dick and Thea, who fell into step with him to hear what he had to say. "They were all on Nym's bankroll. Now I've got half the cops in the city here to help because every Typo Squad agent is down at the Grammatica, doing as much as they can. Including those three recruits we met the other day on the range. Between you, me, and the lamppost, I wouldn't be surprised if we never see any of them again once they get a taste of CLIT life."

"You'll certainly never see Big again," Dick said.

Tanka stopped and gave them both a serious look. "We've got to catch this guy, Dick. And I mean now. Do you have any ideas?"

"Well," Dick said, but he looked hesitant. "There is one more person I could talk to."

"Who?" asked Tanka.

"Miss Information," Dick replied.

"Oh, Jesus."

"Who's Miss Information?" Thea asked.

"She's an old friend," Dick answered.

"Ah," Thea said, nodding sagely. "At this point, I know what that means."

"She's in charge of Mot Grange," Tanka said.

"What's Mot Grange?" asked Thea.

"The local gentlemen's establishment," Dick said.

Thea thought for a moment, and then a look of understanding crossed her face. "She's a madam at a whorehouse?" she said incredulously.

"Well," Dick said. "Yeah."

"If you leave now, you should get there just when things are most lively," Tanka said.

Dick nodded, turning to Thea. "You want to stay here?"

"Are you kidding me?" Thea asked. "There is *no way* I'm missing this."

They drove on long, darkened back roads for nearly an hour before Thea finally spoke. "This looks like a good area to bring somebody if you're planning on killing them."

"Miss Information does value her privacy," Dick said. "And so do her clients. Rumor has it that His Honor the mayor himself is quite adept at navigating these very roads."

"Really?" Thea said. "The mayor?"

"That's what I hear."

"Isn't he married?"

"Yep. With five kids."

"Well, he's a healthy boy, I'll give him that."

The road banked into a steep climb and they passed under an archway of ancient, gnarled trees. “How much longer until we get there?” Thea asked.

The words had just come out of her mouth when they reached a clearing and saw an ornate fountain bubbling in front of an ancient, proud mansion. Warm light spilled onto the porch from the frosted glass of the front doors, and shiny black shutters hid whatever was happening in the upstairs rooms. Even from a distance, they could hear festive music, shouts, and laughter coming from within.

Dick parked in the turnout, and he and Thea approached the front door. He rang the doorbell, and a curvaceous silhouette approached from the other side. The door opened and a stunning brunette in black-and-red lingerie stood in the doorway.

“Oh, hi Dick,” she said brightly. She eyed Thea up and down. “Bringing in some new talent for the boss to check out?”

“Hey!” Thea said indignantly.

“No, nothing like that,” Dick cut across

them. "This is my new partner. I just need to ask the boss a few questions. Is she available?"

The girl looked at Dick and batted her fake eyelashes. "Oh, Dick," she said. "She always has time for you. She *makes* time for you. Come on in."

They passed through the expansive hallway and into a waiting area appointed in fine polished oak, brass, and antique furniture. Scattered around the place, sitting and standing, were girls of every shape and size, in various stages of undress, eyeing them both hungrily. Thea edged closer to Dick, who paid the women no mind at all.

They passed a set of open double doors on the right that gave way to a bar. Dick looked in and saw even more women entertaining a host of gentlemen callers. At a glance, Dick recognized the Semicolons' third baseman, Justin from the firing range, and the mayor, all drinking and having a ball.

They reached a wide, circular room at the end of the hallway. A door opened with a theatrical flourish, and out stepped Miss

Information. She was a big, buxom blonde with a knowing twinkle in her eye and a practiced smile on her bright red lips. She wore a long black silk gown that hugged her body in a way that was just short of obscene. She kept her expression neutral, but when she saw Dick her face brightened all the same.

"Hello, Richard," she said in a deep, throaty husk.

"I prefer Dick."

"Then you might be in the wrong place," Miss Information said quickly, and the girls around the room tittered.

"You look good," Dick said. "It's been a while since I saw you in person."

"Well whose fault is that?" She sidled up as close to him as she could, tapping the tip of his nose with her finger. "I'm here every night; you know that. But you always pick one of my girls instead. Why is that?"

"Because I can't afford you," he said.

The girls all laughed again, and this time Miss Information joined them.

"Listen, I need your help with something. Can we talk in private?" He gestured toward the door to her chambers.

"Dick," she said, "we can do anything you like in private." She hooked his arm and began guiding him away.

"Wait here," Dick told Thea. She shrugged and sat down carefully between two women lounging on a Queen Anne sofa with effortless grace. Thea blinked at the woman to her left, then turned to the woman on her right. "My goodness. That's certainly a lot of cleavage."

Dick smiled, then let Miss Information lead him away.

Miss Information led Dick into a room dominated by the single biggest bed he'd ever seen. The candles on every free surface gave the room a soft, flickering glow, and the assorted cuffs and clips hanging on the walls gleamed weakly.

"You've redecorated," Dick said.

"Well, I needed to replace the bed." She patted the duvet gently. "The old one just wasn't . . . durable enough. So I reappointed the whole room while I was at it. What do you think?"

"It's nice," Dick said. "Cozy."

"Glad you like it."

"Has Anton Nym seen it?"

He expected her to be shocked, or angry, or thrown off in some manner, but instead she smiled and swatted at him playfully. "Dick!" she said. "Just like that? No foreplay even?"

"Sorry." He grinned in spite of himself. "I'm a bit pressed for time."

"Well, if you're planning to get anything out of me, you're going to have to play first," she said.

"Really?"

"Oh, come on, Dick," she said. "It's been ages. You're the best I ever had. Don't make me beg."

Dick took a deep breath and sighed. "All right. But as soon as we're done, you'll tell me what you know. Deal?"

"Deal!" she squealed. "Take off your jacket and get on the bed. I'll be right back."

She slipped off through a small doorway and disappeared. Dick slipped off his jacket and crawled onto the bed, sinking deep into the marshmallow mattress.

"Are you ready?" she called from the other room.

"Yes."

"Then let's do it." She walked back into the room, and in her hands was a Scrabble board.

The board was set between them, and Miss Information was as giddy as a schoolgirl. Anytime Dick tried to bring up anything about Nym, she shushed him and insisted he continue playing.

"Listen, my partner's been waiting a long time," Dick said at last, when the board was nearly full.

"Oh, I'm sure she's fine. My girls will keep her well entertained."

Dick smiled at the thought of Thea being entertained by Miss Information's girls, and played the word QUAY off the Y in ESSAY.

"Very nice," Miss Information said. She looked at her tray of letters, and then looked up at Dick. They locked eyes, and she placed the tiles on the board without looking at them.

Dick looked down. She had placed tiles around the Q in QUAY to spell AQUATIC. But she spelled it AQATIC. The euphoric disorientation hit him almost immediately.

"What . . . ?" was all he could manage before the room began to spin. He got awkwardly to his feet, shaking his head in an effort to sluff the effects, but if anything, it only made them worse.

He looked over at Miss Information. She was wavy, off kilter, but he could see that she was watching him impassively, neither inclined to help him nor particularly concerned about his plight.

The room kept shifting like a funhouse ride. He held on as long as he could, but darkness filled his vision and he pitched forward on the bed, knocking the Scrabble board sideways and sending the pieces flying.

As he drifted somewhere between unconsciousness and consciousness, Dick became aware of a muted voice speaking in the background.

"Okay," the voice was saying. It sounded like a record that had been slowed down to the wrong speed. "I'll take care of it."

Then Dick felt a soft hand on his forehead, and everything slowly came back. Miss Information had typoed him.

He opened his eyes and saw his reflection in the mirror over the bed. Miss Information was curled up next to him, and as he watched, she moved her hand gently from his forehead to his cheeks.

"Dick?" she asked, and to his ears, her voice had returned to normal. "Are you all right?"

He sat up too quickly and paid for it. A painful stab split his brain, followed by a deep, rhythmic pounding. He fell back onto the duvet and put his hand over his eyes.

"Urgh," he managed.

"Sorry, my sweet, wonderful man," Miss Information said. "I hated to have to do that."

"Then why did you?" Dick muttered. His voice sounded much too deep to his ears.

"It's just business, Dick," she replied.

"Strictly business."

He slowly opened his eyes again and looked at her. She batted her eyelashes and smiled, her dazzlingly white teeth contrasting with her bright red lipstick.

"Business?" Dick croaked.

"That's all," Miss Information said. "I had to knock you out for a short while so I could call him."

"Call who?" Dick asked.

She rolled her eyes. "Who do you think?"

Dick suddenly felt much more awake and alert, though he could feel his temples still pulsing with his hangover. He sat up again, more slowly this time, and regarded her.

"Nym?" he asked. "You called Nym? Why?"

"He said if you showed up, to let him know," she said simply, shrugging. "Like I said, business."

"Okay, we're gonna need to go back to the beginning, here. How do you know Anton Nym?"

"Oh, now," Miss Information said, sitting up and scooting over to the edge of the bed.

"If there's one thing you should know about me by now, Dick, is that I don't give it away for free."

Dick sighed deeply. He reached into his pocket, pulled out his wallet, and removed a $100 bill. He handed it to Miss Information, who made it vanish into her ample cleavage.

She hesitated, as if unsure what to say or how much. "Mot Grange is experiencing . . . financial difficulties. I don't have nearly as many clients as I had even six months ago. I blame happy families."

"Go on," said Dick.

"Well, I put out a few feelers and found a financial backer who was willing to help me out."

"Anton Nym."

"Yes," Miss Information said plainly. "Anton Nym."

"And in exchange for the loan, he asked you to rat me out?"

"Let's choose our words carefully, Dick," she replied. "The money wasn't a loan. It was a gift. And I didn't *rat you out.* It's not like he's coming here to kill you or anything."

"Oh, well, that's reassuring." Dick got unsteadily to his feet. He stepped on several Scrabble tiles, but didn't seem to notice. Then a thought occurred to him.

"Did you meet him in person?" Dick asked.

Miss Information smiled and batted her eyelashes again.

"Oh for Christ's sake," Dick said, digging another $100 bill from his wallet. He threw it on the bed, and she made it disappear as well.

"Of course I met him," she said. "A man offers you that much money, the least you can do is shake his hand. Or any other body part he prefers."

"I'm guessing you didn't see his face," Dick said. "He was wearing a mask? Silver asterisk in the middle of the forehead?"

"Yes."

"Did the fact that you were making a financial deal with a man in a mask strike you as . . . I don't know, unusual?" Dick asked.

"Honey, in my line of work, 'unusual' is a very loose term."

"Fair enough," Dick said. "Let's get to the

phone call. What did he say when you told him I was here?"

"That, my dear, you can have for free," she said. "He gave me two messages to give you. One now, and one later."

"Messages?"

"Messages," she repeated.

There was silence between them for a moment. "Well?" he demanded.

"See what your brother knows," she said.

"What?" Dick asked, completely thrown by the change in direction. "What does my brother have to do with any of this? Come on, what's the message?"

"I just gave it to you," Miss Information said. "The message is: See what your brother knows."

Dick stared at her blankly. "What the hell is that supposed to mean?"

"I'm just the messenger," Miss Information said. "But if you'd like to hear my opinion . . ."

Dick hesitated, but decided he needed all the help he could get. He pulled another $100 bill out of his wallet, handing it over.

"In my opinion," she said, "he wants you to go and see what your brother knows."

Dick rolled his eyes. "You're a big help. What's the other message?"

"Ah-ah-ah," she said, holding up her finger and wagging it playfully at him. "One now, one later, remember?"

"But when is later?"

"I have a feeling you'll know when later is." She sat down primly on the edge of the bed. "And I'll be right here waiting when you do."

"Always a pleasure," Dick said. He made his way through the door leading to Miss Information's chambers and back out into the circular room at the end of the hallway.

"Thea?" he called, but she was nowhere to be seen. A blonde woman in a red satin robe sat on a nearby lounge, making bedroom eyes at Dick.

"Have you seen my partner?" he asked her.

"No," she said seductively. "But I'll be your partner if you like."

Dick crossed through an archway into

another lounge area, where he heard music and raucous laughter coming from behind a closed door. He opened it.

It was a wide, mirrored room. Multicolored lights flashed off the walls, and a disco ball twirled on the ceiling. In the center of the room was a stripper pole, and all of Miss Information's ladies were gathered around it, yelling and applauding.

Glued to the pole was Thea, doing her best to look seductive and sexual in her black Typo Squad uniform. As Dick watched, she hooked a leg around the top part of the pole and swung herself in a wide arc, arms spread wide and fingertips extended. The women watching exploded with cheers and applause. Dick approached the pole.

Thea was in the middle of a long, complicated one-legged twirl when Dick joined the audience, his arms folded, his head cocked slightly to the side. As Thea finished her maneuver and threw up her arms in victory, to renewed excitement from the women watching, she spotted Dick. She jumped awkwardly off the pole as though it had suddenly become electrified and stood there, looking abashed.

The women watching burst into a chorus of boos as the routine ended, and Dick took several steps forward. "What exactly are you doing?" he shouted over the still-throbbing music.

Thea looked over at the pole and then back at him. "Blending in," she shouted back.

Dick grinned, offering his hand to help her down from the small stage surrounding the pole. The other women hugged her and high-fived her as they moved through the crowd.

"We have some work to do," he told her as they headed to the lobby. "Unless you have a midnight show you need to be here for."

She punched him playfully on the shoulder. "So what did that fat old whore have to say?" she asked, nodding her head toward Miss Information's chambers.

"Hey now," Dick said reproachfully, and then paused to process what Thea had just said. "She's not . . . old. She's my age."

Thea opened her mouth gleefully to reply, but Dick held up a finger of warning.

"Don't!"

"You ruin all my fun, Dick," Thea said as they passed through the front doors and out into the darkness beyond. "So really, what did she say?"

Dick filled her in on everything that had happened. Thea listened intently, then shook her head.

"Did it occur to you that you could've used her phone to call Nym?" she said, exasperated. "Maybe had a trace put on it? Find out where he's hiding?"

"Hey, that fat old whore isn't stupid," Dick replied. "She'd have thought of that."

"So we're going to Fula Ord?" Thea asked as they climbed into the SUV.

"Unless you have a better idea," Dick said.

CHAPTER ELEVEN

Dick was uncharacteristically quiet as they drove north, passing through stately neighborhoods and frowning brownstones. Thea left him alone.

"It's been a while since I've seen him," he said suddenly, breaking the steady hum of the engine. "Chicago, I mean."

"Oh?" Thea asked.

"Yeah," Dick said. "I used to visit him a lot early on. I was kind of hoping he might come back, but whenever I tried to talk to him, he only spoke in riddles and weird, disconnected phrases. A few doctors thought they could help him and they tried a lot of therapy and put him on a bunch of different drug trials. But none of it ever did any good."

They turned off the main street and joined a wide, sweeping driveway that led to Fula Ord. The grounds were immaculate, the grass so brightly green it hurt Thea's eyes to look at it, but the building itself was nothing remarkable. Just a brick facade with tinted windows. It could just as easily have been a dentist's office or a middle school.

They pulled up to the front door and Dick got out. "Are you sure you want to do this?" he asked.

"I'm sure," Thea said. "And I'll stay with you this time. I doubt there are any stripper poles here."

"You might be surprised," Dick said.

They ascended the stairs to the entryway.

After they both signed in and presented their IDs, the nurse at the reception desk told them to have a seat. The small, dingy waiting room overflowed with out-of-date magazines and crushed paper cups. In the corner, a balding man in a thin blue robe and paper slippers sat on the edge of his chair, grabbing wildly at the air above him, as if bedeviled by invisible butterflies.

Twenty minutes went by, and then a steel door across the room buzzed loudly and an extremely attractive woman in a white coat with a clipboard stepped out and looked around.

"Mister Shonnary?" she called. "Miss Saurus?"

Dick and Thea stood and crossed the room to meet her.

"Good morning," the woman said, a little stiffly. "I'm Doctor Paye. Mister Manuel is a patient of mine. Follow me, please."

She stepped aside so Dick and Thea could pass, then closed the door tightly behind her. The three of them fell in step together, making their way down a long, tiled, brightly lit corridor. They passed multiple rooms along the way. In one, a woman who looked even younger than Thea bumped her head softly against the wall, naming off state capitals with every hit. In another, an older man sat in a wheelchair, furiously shaking his head, as if strongly disagreeing with unheard voices. Still another held a woman who looked to be in her eighties, who was singing show tunes at the top of her lungs while whipping off her hospital gown with a stripper's flourish. A weary-looking orderly gathered up the gown, perhaps to try and get it back on her.

At the end of the corridor, they turned into a small office, where Dick and Thea took seats on the opposite side of Doctor Paye's desk.

"So," Doctor Paye began, "I understand you're here to visit your brother."

"That's right," Dick said.

The doctor thumbed through some paperwork on her desk. "According to this, it's been more than three years since your last visit." It was less of a statement and more of an accusation.

"If that's what it says," Dick replied. "That sounds about right."

"So why now, if I may ask?"

"I'm not sure that's any of your concern," Thea piped up. "If Dick wants to visit his brother, why does the reason matter?"

Doctor Paye leaned back in her chair, studying Thea over her dark-framed glasses.

Then she turned to Dick. "Mister Shonnary, I've been working with Chicago for the past eighteen months, and in that time we've made what I believe to be significant progress. We've also gotten close. He's trusted me with a lot of his most significant concerns and fears."

"It was my understanding that none of the doctors here had been able to reach my brother on any level," Dick said. Now *he* had the tone of accusation. "I wonder how you were able to do so."

"Well," she replied, "some doctors just have a better rapport with their patients. And frankly, some doctors are more skilled than others."

"So that's how you reached him?" Thea said with a grin. "Your skills?"

The doctor's eyes narrowed. Thea's grin grew ever wider.

"Look, I appreciate what you've done for my brother," Dick said, "but we're wasting time here. I need to see him."

"Frankly, Mister Shonnary, I don't feel that's in Chicago's best interests," Doctor

Paye said baldly.

"Why not?"

The doctor seemed to be weighing her words carefully. "Normally I wouldn't be able to discuss these matters because of doctor-patient confidentiality," she said. "But in this case, and since you're family, I'm going to make an exception. I believe seeing you could undo much of the work I've done in my time with him. You see, he blames you for his being here."

Dick's lips tightened. The words he spoke at Merriam's bar came floating back to him. *It was my fault. He never wanted this life. I talked him into it.*

"I'm afraid," she continued, "Chicago feels that as his older brother, you should have tried to dissuade him from joining Typo Squad. If you had, he could've lived a long and happy life, far away from Fula Ord."

"There's no way I could've known what was going to happen to him," Dick said defensively. "When you join Typo Squad, you know the risks and you accept them. Chicago was no different."

"That may well be, Mister Shonnary," Doctor Paye said. "But as his physician, I need to do what's best for Chicago. And I believe seeing you will cause him unnecessary stress and mental anguish. I'm afraid I have to deny your request."

"And I'm afraid you have no jurisdiction in this matter, doctor," Dick said, his temper rising. "I'm his only living relative, and you have no legal grounds to keep me from seeing him."

"Has anything I've said here gotten through to you?" the doctor replied. "I'm telling you that you could cause him significant developmental setbacks. Is that what you want for him?"

"Of course not. But I'm trying to stop a mass murderer, and Chicago is the only lead I have."

The doctor's brow furrowed. "What possible information could he have that would be relevant?"

"I don't know."

"Well then what led you to him in the first place?"

"We have . . . an informant," Dick said at last. "She told me to come visit him, but didn't say why."

"And on the strength of that, you want me to let you see him?" Doctor Paye scoffed.

Dick took a deep breath. "Look. I realize it doesn't make a whole lot of sense, but we're grasping at straws here, and I feel we may be running out of time."

"I'm sorry, Mister Shonnary—" she began, but he cut her off.

"Five minutes," he said. "Just give me five minutes with him. Then we'll go, I promise. Please."

Ten minutes later, Dick and Thea sat in the institution's drab cafeteria. The cracked plastic chairs and shabby linoleum tables reminded Dick of the public schools he'd attended in his youth. There were no patients, but a handful of white-coated orderlies sat at a nearby table, talking softly.

A door behind them opened, and Doctor Paye appeared, leading a tall, disheveled, shuffling figure into the room. Dick stood, marveling at the difference in his brother.

Chicago had always been a broad, solid man with skin that looked perpetually tanned and a shock of thick black hair. Now he was thin, not just in his body but in his arms, shoulders, and face. It was as though the man Dick had known had been drained. His hair stood up in every direction, and had gone a bright white at the temples. His skin had paled under the fluorescent lights, and looked like it no longer fit his skull properly.

Doctor Paye guided Chicago to a chair at the table. Dick sat down as well. Thea squeezed Dick's shoulder reassuringly.

Chicago was looking around the room, but mostly at the ceiling. He carefully avoided looking anywhere in Dick's general direction. An awful silence built between them.

"Hey, Chicago," Dick said at last.

"Chicago," his brother croaked. "Third most populous city in the United States. Derived from a French rendering of the Native American word *shikaakwa*, meaning 'wild leek' in the Miami-Illinois language. Good hockey team."

"Yeah," Dick said, smiling in spite of himself. "But I don't mean the city Chicago. I mean you. Chicago. Do you know who I am?"

"Richard Shonnary," he said without hesitation. "You prefer Dick. Running joke."

"Good," Dick said.

"And that's Thea Saurus," Chicago said, pointing at Thea, but not looking at her. "She likes blueberry Pop-Tarts. Her tic is that she comes when she sees a typo."

Dick, Thea, and Doctor Paye exchanged glances.

"How did you know that?" Dick asked incredulously.

"I know what I know," Chicago said airily, still looking around the room.

"Listen, I don't have much time, and I need to ask you about something," Dick said.

"Yeah," Chicago said. "Anton Nym."

Dick felt a painful surge of adrenaline hit his veins, and the hair on the back of his neck stood up. "That's . . . that's right. What do you know about Anton Nym?"

Chicago finally swiveled his head down and looked Dick dead in the eyes. He had a sudden focus, an intensity that Dick hadn't seen since they were both very young men.

"You'll never catch him," Chicago said simply.

"Why not?" Dick said.

It all happened in a heartbeat. Chicago jumped up, kicked over his chair, and pushed Dick down on the linoleum by the lapels of his jacket. His eyes were wild, bulging, and spittle flew from his lips.

"Because he's too smart for you!" Chicago screamed. Dick heard the squeaking footsteps of the orderlies coming toward them and random voices shouting.

"He'll ruin you!" Chicago continued. "He'll destroy everything you've worked for! And there's nothing! Anybody! Can do about it!"

Chicago was yanked roughly off of him and dragged backward. As quickly as the rage had come on him, it was gone, and he was once again the calm, placid patient who had entered the room only minutes before.

"Please escort Mister Manuel back to his room," Doctor Paye breathlessly instructed the orderlies on either side of him. "I'll be there shortly."

The trio left, and Thea helped Dick to his feet.

"Well?" Doctor Paye said, her breathing fast. "Satisfied?"

"Not by a long shot," Dick said. "There's no way he could've known those things. Someone in here has been feeding him information."

"To what end?" Doctor Paye said. "If you hadn't come here today, what was he going to do with all that he knows? Post it in a blog? Leak it to the press? You saw him. He's only now coming back from the damage he suffered. All I can say is that I hope you haven't caused a permanent regression. Now if you don't mind, I have matters to attend to. You can show yourselves out."

She left without another word.

In the driveway a few minutes later, Dick stopped next to the SUV to confer with Thea.

"What do you think?" Thea asked.

"I have no idea what to think," Dick said.

"But there's something going on here. I just don't know how we're supposed to find out what it is."

"Well," Thea offered, "Miss Information said she's got another message for you, right? Maybe now it's time to find out what it is."

Dick smiled at her. "That's an excellent idea." He dug out his phone and called Miss Information's number.

"Hello, Dick," the sultry voice on the other end said. "Miss me already?"

"Like I miss my tonsils," Dick replied. "You've got another message for me?"

"Oh yes."

Silence on the line.

"Well?" Dick prodded.

"I'm afraid I can only give it to you in person, Dick," Miss Information said. "See you soon."

Dick looked wide-eyed at Thea.

"What?" She sounded alarmed. "What is it?"

"She's making us go back to Mot Grange," Dick said incredulously.

"*What?*"

"Let's stop by headquarters and get Tanka caught up first." Dick slammed the SUV into gear, jamming on the gas pedal.

"That fat old whore," Thea muttered, shaking her head.

They arrived back at headquarters a short while later, and as they passed through the lobby toward Autumn's desk, they saw Scott Shwiski heading toward them, looking extremely sour.

"Hey there, handsome!" Dick called brightly.

Shwiski looked up and saw them. He sneered.

"What brings you by?" Dick continued. "Forget your Typo Squad Agent of the Month award in your locker?"

Autumn, eavesdropping on the conversation, filled the lobby with her trademark howling laughter.

"I was here to provide my rock-solid alibis," Shwiski said, his words clipped. He shook his head. "You people really thought I could be him, didn't you?"

Dick took a step toward him. "You're lucky you're not," he said softly, "or I'd kill you where you stand."

Shwiski smirked, unimpressed. "Good luck catching him," he said. "You'll be seeing me again real soon. *Dick*."

He continued on his way toward the main entrance.

"Don't let the door hit your ass on the way out!" Autumn cried suddenly. Without looking back, Shwiski gave her the finger, then was gone.

"What an asshole," Autumn muttered, and returned to her work.

Once inside, Dick was surprised to see the entire team waiting for him and Thea in the office area.

"I thought you were all helping out at the Grammatica," Dick said.

"We were," Big said dreamily. "Oh, that's a cushy gig. I was looking over some copy in my soft fluffy robe and one of the support staff gave me a foot massage and did my cuticles. I've been wasting my life in Typo

Squad!"

"You've been wasting our lives, too," Ewan quipped.

"I was able to get a hold of Typo Corps down in Escondido," Tanka told Dick. "They sent up some of their reserves to relieve these guys. But never mind that. What's going on?"

Dick quickly recounted everything that had happened at Mot Grange and Fula Ord.

"So then why bother sending you all the way over to see Chicago?" Anna asked. "What purpose did it serve?"

"That's what I'm going to find out," Dick said.

"We're coming with you," Tanka said.

"All right! It's a caper!" Big exclaimed.

CHAPTER TWELVE

They pulled into Mot Grange in the late afternoon. The mansion was quiet and peaceful, all evidence of the revelry from the previous night swept away.

"Mot Grange," Big said wistfully, getting out of the SUV behind Anna. "I had the single greatest night of my life here."

"Oh?" asked Ewan, climbing out behind him. "Was it all-you-can-eat buffalo wings night?"

Big scowled at him. "I hate you," he said plainly. "But yes, it was."

"C'mon," Dick said, leading the way to the front doors. He entered the deserted lobby with the team behind him. Bright streaks of late-day sunlight shone across the Persian rugs, cutting them in swatches of light and dark red. The place was silent, but as they made their way further in, scantily clad women began to appear in doorways, watching them with catlike curiosity.

They reached the door that led to Miss Information's chambers.

"Wait here," Dick instructed the team.

"Uh . . . yeah, we can do that," Big stammered as the women who had been watching them now approached with bright smiles. "Take your time."

Dick made his way through the door. Once again the candles were all lit, casting the room in a soft orange glow. Miss Information lay on her side on the enormous bed, wearing a lacy black dressing gown over matching lingerie.

"What took you so long?" she purred.

"I had to swing by the bank," Dick said. "Pick up some more hundreds in case you decided to charge me for more tidbits."

Miss Information pouted. "You make me out to be such a bad girl."

"My apologies." He sat down on the edge

of the bed. "You're a saint."

"Oh, now I wouldn't go that far," she said, her smile returning.

"So. You have the second message for me?"

"I do."

"May I have it, please?"

"Thanks," Miss Information said simply.

"For what?" Dick asked.

"That's the second message," she replied. "Thanks."

"What does that mean?"

Miss Information shrugged. "That's all he told me, Dick," she said. "Sorry. That's all I know."

Back out in the circular room at the end of the hallway, Dick rejoined the team. He chased off the women who had parked themselves on the laps of Ewan, Big, and Tanka, and gathered everyone in a tight circle to tell them what he'd learned.

"Thanks?" Big said. "She made you come all the way back out here just to tell you that?"

"She's a unique one," Dick said. "She always has been. But what does it mean?"

"Okay, let's go over it," Anna said. "You came here, and she gave you the first message from Nym, which was 'See what your brother knows,' right?"

"Right," Dick agreed.

"So that drove you to go and visit Chicago in Fula Ord," Anna continued. "But that turned out to be a waste of time, and then she demanded that you come back here so that she could give you the second message, which was 'Thanks.'"

Before she'd even finished, Dick's eyes widened, his face turning a bright pink.

"He wanted to find Chicago," Dick whispered. He turned to Thea with desperation in his eyes. "He didn't know where Chicago was, so he used the first message to send me there. He must have followed us. Now he knows he's in Fula Ord, and he's had more than enough time to get to him."

"Oh God," Thea said. "We led that psychotic bastard right to him. That's why Nym's thanking you."

Dick spun on his heel and ran for the

front door. The rest of the team launched themselves after him, exploding out onto the front lawn and heading straight for the SUV. Tanka had his phone out.

"I want every available officer to converge on Fula Ord," he said. "Have them set up a perimeter. No one leaves. And under no circumstances does anyone go in there until I arrive, is that understood?"

He hung up and nodded to Dick, who had jumped behind the wheel.

"He'll be okay, Dick," Thea said reassuringly from the passenger seat. "He'll be okay."

Dick nodded, but didn't look convinced.

Dick floored the gas pedal all the way back to Fula Ord, sirens wailing and lights flashing, with dozens of other police cars joining him, wailing and flashing as his escort. They zipped through red lights and narrowly missed clipping one vehicle after another. The rest of the team bounced around in the back while Thea held onto the passenger side door for dear life, and more than once pumped an imaginary brake.

By the time they all arrived at Fula Ord, the sun had fully set. The place was dark and silent, and the only illumination came from the police lights that bounced off the darkened building. Cops in standard uniform, along with others in riot gear, and still others with automatic weapons, took up their positions and waited for orders.

Dick got out of the SUV and unholstered his weapon. Thea, Big, Ewan, Anna, and Tanka did the same, and they gathered in a small circle on the lawn out in front of the main entrance.

Dick turned to Tanka. "How do you want to do this?"

"Whatever way doesn't get everyone killed," he said. "You and Thea take point. The rest of you line up in cover formation behind him. We need to make sure Nym doesn't have any typo-related surprises before we send the rest of the force in. Dick, keep me updated, okay?"

Dick nodded. "Let's move."

They moved into the wide-open front doors and found themselves in the darkened waiting room. Dick peered over the front desk. Both nurses who had been working there were dead, fresh bullet holes in their foreheads. He peeked around the corner. The patient he'd seen earlier grabbing at imaginary butterflies was dead as well.

Dick motioned them forward. The thick steel door leading into the rest of the building was open, and they moved cautiously through it. Flashlights flicked on as they made their way into the main corridor.

The silence was suffocating. Dick moved slowly forward, Thea on his right, the rest of the team moving in behind them.

They came to the first set of patient rooms and Dick held up his fist. Everyone dropped to one knee and assumed a shooter's stance, their weapons all held at high port. Dick leaned forward, peering into the room on his right. The only light came from moonlight streaming through the bars in a high-set window, but it was enough to see that the old man sitting in his wheelchair was dead. But he hadn't been shot.

In the faint glow, Dick could see the word CATAGORY scrawled in huge red letters on the wall opposite the victim.

Dick looked away as quickly as he could, but still felt a wave of dizziness pass over him. He felt Anna's hand on his shoulder, and he nodded to let her know he was all right. With quick hand gestures, he silently warned the rest of the team that all of the rooms likely had typos and to proceed with caution.

They moved on, with Dick only glancing in the rooms now, but every patient appeared to have died by typo. At the end of the corridor, another hallway cut across, so they could go either left or right.

Again, Dick gestured to indicate that Thea and Ewan should go left with him, and Big and Anna should head right. He also pointed to his earpiece, indicating that if anything went wrong, they should call. Nods all around, and Dick, Thea, and Ewan forged ahead.

They came to a set of double doors with a keycard lock, but the doors were chocked open by a wheelchair. Thea held the door as Dick rolled the chair out of the way, and they found themselves in a carpeted hallway with a less industrial feel.

The rooms down here were all offices—some for doctors, some for administrators, and others for support staff. Dick, Thea, and Ewan glanced in them as they passed, but they were exactly the same as the patient rooms. Not a single soul alive.

A sudden burst of static in Dick's earpiece brought them all to a sudden halt.

"Big?" Dick whispered. "Big? Are you all right?"

"Motherfucker!" came Big's filtered voice.

Dick looked at Thea and Ewan, and they all knew what it meant in an instant. They jumped up and ran through the double doors, passing the intersection with the main hallway and following the corridor that Big and Anna had taken.

"Dick!" came Tanka's voice through the earpiece. "Dick, what's going on?"

"Big!" Dick shouted, no longer caring whether or not they were heard, ignoring

Tanka. "Big!"

"Cocksucker!" came Big's voice again, only this time it echoed through their earpieces and down the hallway.

"Shit!" Big said. He was getting louder as they moved in closer. "Asshole!"

The three of them rounded a final corner and stopped dead.

It was another short hallway leading into a cavernous room, and unlike the rest of the building, the lights were on. Scrawled in jagged red letters on every surface—walls, floor, ceiling, everywhere—were typos.

RECIEVE said one. VALENTIME'S DAY said another. FOURTY. AQUAINTANCE. GUIDENCE. INDEPENDANT. LIASON. There was nowhere to look without seeing one.

Big stood rooted to the spot where the corridor met the room. "Dildos!" he shouted. "Douchebag!" Anna was on her knees next to him, her arms wrapped around her midsection, vomiting copiously.

Before Dick realized what was happening, he felt the whole room go hazy and out of focus. He was suddenly euphoric, and laughed as Thea tried to catch him as he tumbled to his knees. He heard Thea's moan and heavy breathing on one side of him and Ewan's high-pitched, hysterical giggling on the other. None of them had ever been exposed to so many typos in one place at one time before.

Dick fought with all his might to stay conscious, but it was no use. He slipped into darkness, hearing Big shout "Bugfucker!" as he did.

The first thing he was aware of was shallow, quick breathing next to him. Dick was slowly making his way back to consciousness, but it was a slippery eel he couldn't quite grab. He focused on the breathing as an anchor, a touchstone back to the real world.

His eyes wouldn't open just yet, but at least he was *aware* of his eyes. That was something. In fact, the left one itched, and as he reached up to scratch it, it came to him that his arms were tied down. The shallow breathing continued, like a woman riding the first real contraction of childbirth.

He forced his eyes open and looked around.

He was in a padded cell, seated on the floor across from the door, which was wide open. He tried to move his hand again, and realized he was in a straightjacket, wrapping his arms tight around his torso.

He turned to his right, where the shallow breathing was coming from. There was his brother, on the floor right next to him, in his own straightjacket, and his eyes were wide with panic. He was hyperventilating.

"Chicago?" Dick asked blearily. "What's going on?"

"He's—gonna—kill—me," Chicago wheezed with each panicked breath.

The look of terror on Chicago's face was like a splash of cold water.

"Who?" Dick asked.

"Nym," Chicago answered. "Don't—want—to—die."

"Okay, listen to me," Dick said. "Chicago? I need you to listen. I'm going to get you out of here, okay? No one's going to kill you today."

"Can't—get—out."

"The door's wide open," Dick said. "Come on, come with me."

He rolled to his side and got his legs under him. As he pushed up off the floor, the straightjacket suddenly tightened, and he was yanked back down. He looked over at Chicago's straightjacket and saw a chain running from it to the wall behind him.

"Huh," Dick said. "All right, we'll have to do this the hard way." He began twisting his shoulders, trying to get his arms loose.

Suddenly Chicago's breathing intensified, though it didn't seem possible. "Too—late," he wheezed.

Dick looked up and saw two burly, white-coated orderlies enter the cell. One of them unhooked the chain holding Chicago to the wall and then the two of them hoisted him to his feet. Chicago began to struggle, digging in the heels of his bare feet on the faded linoleum floor.

"Hey!" Dick shouted. "Hey! Let him go!"

Chicago made grunting noises and

whimpered as the orderlies dragged him forward. He was thrashing as much as he could, which wasn't much.

"Dick!" he called over his shoulder. "*Dick!*"

He was dragged into the shadows of the hallway beyond the cell. Dick could only make out the fading outlines of the orderlies' uniforms.

"Chicago!" Dick twisted frantically, straining as hard as he could against his confinement, but it was no use. He wasn't making any progress.

"Chicago!" he called again, leaning forward so he could brace his feet on the wall behind him and push with his legs against the chain. It had no effect, other than to make the straightjacket even tighter.

Dick could hear his brother jibbering from down the hallway, and then there was a metallic clunk, as if a door opened.

"Noooooo," Chicago cried pitifully. "*Noooooo!*"

There was a horrible silence that seemed to hold its own eternity as Dick strained to hear what was happening.

Then a chilling scream of agony filled the hallway.

"*Gaaaaaaaaaaaaahhhhhhhgh*!"

The sound filled Dick's veins with ice water. It held for nearly half a minute, then cut short. It was followed by another echoing silence.

Dick was numb with shock. He slumped back against the wall behind him and stared straight into nothingness.

"Chicago," he said, barely a whisper.

He didn't know how long he sat there. Minutes seemed to stretch to years as he turned it over repeatedly in his mind. His brother was dead, and there had been nothing he could do to stop it.

He barely registered the sound of footsteps approaching the cell. When he looked up, a figure stood in the doorway. He was dressed in an impeccable black suit with a purple carnation in the buttonhole. His face was obscured by a black mask, a silver asterisk gleaming in the center of the forehead.

"You," Dick spat.

"A genuine pleasure seeing you again, Richard," Nym said cheerfully, though his voice was still distorted. "Comfortable?"

"Anton Nym," Dick said, still struggling against his bonds, "you are under arrest."

"Oh my," Nym said. "Whatever for?"

"Killing my brother," Dick said gravely, "for a start."

"Yes, well, you see, you can't really arrest me for that." Nym crouched down so his face was level with Dick's.

"Fine," Dick said, suddenly furious. "I'm not going to arrest you. I'm going to kill you."

"Please try to understand, Richard," Nym said, now dropping down into a comfortable cross-legged sitting position. "There are things of which you are simply not aware. It was, in fact, utterly necessary to do away with Chicago."

Nym's casual demeanor was making Dick crazy.

Dick's expression turned into a savage grin. "Yeah? Was it utterly necessary to do away with Superscript, too?"

Nym stared at him, suddenly frozen. Only his left eyelid twitched, ever so slightly. Otherwise he might have been a statue.

"What?" Nym said, suddenly bereft of the confidence and swagger with which he'd entered the cell.

Dick lunged forward as far as the chain would allow. "You killed Superscript, you sick son of a bitch!" he howled. "Just a kid, and you shot him dead in the street! You murdered innocent people at the Grammatica, in cold blood!"

Nym turned his head slightly to the left, as though hearing a high-pitched noise that was beyond everyone else's range. His stare was vacant, glassy.

"No," he said, very softly. "No, that's not right."

Dick studied Nym carefully. He suddenly seemed entirely vulnerable, almost childlike. What the hell was going on?

Nym turned back toward Dick. "Did you say—?" he began, but before he could finish, a booming voice filled the hallway behind them.

"Anton Nym!" the voice called. "Let me see your hands! Now!"

A wave of delirious relief spread through Dick's body at the sound of Tanka's voice, still a ways down the corridor, but close enough to have his weapon trained on Nym. He watched as Nym turned and stood, casually raising his hands. Whatever had come over Nym was now gone, and his original swagger seemed to have returned.

"Tanka!" Dick called happily. "You son of a bitch!"

"Dick? You all right?"

"Yeah! Just bag this asshole, will you?"

"Don't worry," Tanka said. "He's not going anywhere."

"Lieutenant Tanka," Nym said, his voice light and friendly. "Welcome. So pleased you could join us."

"Put your hands on your head, turn around, and get on your knees," Tanka commanded. His voice was closer now, though Dick could still only see Nym's outline in the doorway.

"Yes, of course, I'll be delighted to," Nym

said, still in that maddeningly friendly, unconcerned tone. "But before I do, may I ask how you got past the typo room I spent so much time setting up?"

"As it happens," Tanka said, closer still, "I have no tic."

"Really?" Nym said, sounding genuinely interested. "That's fascinating. Exceedingly rare, as I understand it."

"Yeah, well, I'm an exquisite butterfly. It's been great sharing this special moment with you, but now I need you to put your hands on your head—"

"Turn around and get on my knees, yes, I remember," said Nym. "There's just one other thing before I do."

Blam!

The single shot rang out, impossibly loud in the confined silence of the wing. Dick waited for Nym to stagger and fall, but he did neither. He simply put his hands back down at his sides. There was a loud, wet thump in the hallway beyond.

"Thank you," Nym said. "Your timing, as always, is impeccable."

He turned back to face Dick and stepped just inside the doorway. After a moment, Doctor Paye stepped in next to him, holding a large, still-smoking handgun.

"You," Dick whispered.

"No tic," she said to Nym, putting a hand on his shoulder. "I would have loved to study him. A shame, really."

She nodded toward Dick, then turned and looked lovingly at Nym.

"Is everything all right in here, my sweet?" she cooed, placing a finger gently under his chin.

"It is indeed," Nym replied, snaking an arm around the doctor's waist and pulling her close. They smiled at one another.

"Chicago trusted you!" Dick spat at Doctor Paye. "And you let this sick fuck murder him!"

Doctor Paye merely shrugged. Dick thrashed in anger, but his restraints showed no signs of giving.

"Listen, Richard," Nym said, turning his attention back to Dick, "the good doctor and I will be heading out now. Tonight is a truly special night. Do you know why?"

Dick was speechless with rage and numb shock. All he could do was stare.

"It's the anniversary, Richard," Nym said. "Of the night you and Chicago and the rest of your team were on that rooftop. That's where we'll meet you."

A concussive *thud!* vibrated through the floor from somewhere else in the building, followed by shouting voices.

"Time to go," Nym said to Doctor Paye. "See you soon, Richard."

They disappeared through the doorway, and Dick heard another door squeal open and slam.

"Agent Shonnary!" a voice echoed through the building. "Can you hear me?"

"I'm here!" Dick called out, leaning as far forward as the chain would allow. "Down here!"

Multiple footsteps approached. Dick could hear one of the voices calling out to EMTs as they passed Tanka. Two cops ran into the cell, and Dick recognized his old friend Cody, the officer from the baseball stadium.

"Jesus." Cody immediately dropped to his knees and started undoing Dick's restraints.

"Anton Nym and one of the psychologists from this place, Doctor Paye," Dick said quickly. "They just left. Headed out through a fire door, by the sound of it."

The other officer nodded and ran out of the cell. Dick turned to Cody. "Is my team all right?"

"Yeah," Cody said, struggling with the straps that wrapped around Dick's back. "Alive and well. All trussed up, just like you, in another cell."

"How did you guys get in here?" Dick asked. "How did you get past that typo room?"

"Technology," Cody replied. "We sent in a robot with a detonation charge. Blew it up and scorched every surface in that room so no typos were visible."

"Hmph," Dick said.

"What?" Cody untied the final strap.

"Just don't get it in your head that machines are better at dealing with typos than people are," Dick grumbled.

Cody laughed. He pulled the straightjacket off of Dick and helped him to his feet.

"Tanka?" Dick asked soberly.

Cody turned his head to the side and called over his shoulder. "Sullivan!"

"A little busy right now!" a voice called back.

"How's Tanka?"

"Alive!" Sullivan called back. "We're loading him up! I don't know what he's made of, but whatever it is, they should make vests out of it for you guys!"

Dick took a few steps toward the door, then stumbled sideways. Cody caught him before he hit the floor.

"Whoa, easy tiger," Cody said, guiding Dick back to a sitting position. "You've been through a lot. Maybe we should have the EMTs take a look at you, too."

Dick shook his head. "No time. There's someplace I need to be."

"Where?"

"Don't worry about it." He put a bracing hand on Cody's shoulder. "It's a private matter."

More footsteps approached, and Thea, Big, Ewan, and Anna flooded the small cell. They were all sweaty, and Anna had angry red welts on her shoulders, but overall, none of them looked the worse for wear.

"Dick!" Thea cried, and dove into his arms. She held him tight, and he patted her back reassuringly.

"Are you okay?" she asked, releasing him.

"Yeah," he replied. "You guys?"

They all nodded.

"We just saw them wheeling Tanka out," Ewan said gravely. "What happened?"

Dick recounted everything.

"Oh God," Thea said. "I'm so sorry about Chicago."

Dick nodded. "Me, too. But we'll deal with that once Nym is behind bars. Come on, let's get out of here."

Dick led the way out of the cell. He paused to shake Cody's hand. "Thanks for your help, buddy."

"Any time," Cody replied. "Look, if things go sideways wherever it is you're headed, we're only a phone call away."

Dick nodded. He stepped out into the hallway and made his way past a pool of Tanka's smeared blood.

"Where are we going, Dick?" Big asked.

"The library," Dick said simply.

CHAPTER THIRTEEN

The team ran past the crowd of officers gathered out in front of Fula Ord and piled into the SUV. Dick hit the lights and siren, and squealed out of the parking lot, heading toward the sparkling lights of downtown Los Palabras.

"Thea," Dick said, his hands tight on the wheel and his eyes fixed on the fast-rolling road.

"Yeah?"

"I think it's time I told you what happened that night," Dick said evenly. "Five years ago."

He glanced up in the rearview mirror. Ewan, Anna, and Big were all watching him carefully.

"Okay then," Thea said from the passenger seat. "Go ahead."

Dick took a deep breath. "We'd been tracking one of the biggest errorist cells in the country," he began. "Led by a profoundly disturbed woman who called herself Kay Oss. One night, we got a tip that Oss was planning something big, and that she'd set up shop on the roof of the Los Palabras Public Library. Tanka sent us in—me, Chicago, Ewan, Big, Anna, and Red Penny.

"We made our way up to the roof, not really sure what to expect or what we'd find. When we got there, we found Kay Oss standing next to the parapet that overlooked Main Street. She had a line of soldiers on either side of her, and behind them, stacked up all along the edge of the roof, were enormous piles of paper."

"Piles of paper?" Thea asked. "I don't understand."

"She'd printed up thousands and thousands of flyers with some of the worst typos you can imagine on them," Dick said grimly. "If we moved on her, she'd have her men knock the piles over, where they'd float down into the street and into the hands of who knows how many people."

Thea looked stricken. "Jesus," she said softly.

"She was a monster," Ewan said from the back, "but it was a truly brilliant plan. You see, we couldn't shoot her or any of her men for fear that they'd be knocked backward into the flyers, and execute her threat anyway."

"So what happened?" Thea asked. No one seemed inclined to answer.

"Dick, do you want me to tell her?" Big asked kindly.

Dick nodded.

"We were holding fire while Oss did her bad guy speech," Big said. "You know how the more colorful characters love to make their speeches. She was just getting to the part where she was so much smarter than we were and we'd never stop her reign of terror and so forth and so on when . . . someone accidentally fired a shot."

Thea digested this for a moment, and then her eyes went wide with comprehension.

"Chicago," she said simply.

"Yeah," Big nodded. "Chicago."

"So then what?" Thea asked.

Dick picked up the thread of the story. "The guy Chicago accidentally shot did exactly what he was supposed to do," Dick said. "He fell backward and knocked over three huge piles of flyers. Chicago completely froze. In the confusion, the rest of us charged forward and subdued the other soldiers and Kay Oss, but the damage was already done."

"It was a Saturday night," Ewan said. "The streets below were teeming with people. They had no idea the danger that the flyers presented. They picked them up, some snatching them out of the sky. And read them."

"Wait," Thea said suddenly. "You're talking about the Los Palabras Massacre."

"We are indeed," Ewan replied.

"But thousands of people died that night," Thea said. "Are you saying Chicago was responsible?"

Dick nodded.

"Oh, my God," Thea said.

"That was the night Chicago's mind finally snapped," Dick said. "It had been coming for a long time with his undetected tic. But that drove him over the edge. They took him straight to Fula Ord that night, and he's been there ever since." Dick swallowed as realization dawned. "*Had* been there ever since," he corrected.

No one had a response to that.

"So, what, Nym wants to meet you on the same rooftop tonight?" Thea asked. "Why?"

"Tonight's the anniversary of the Los Palabras Massacre," Dick answered. "I don't think it's enough that Nym killed Chicago. I think he wants to rub what happened in my face."

"And what if he just wants to lure you up there to kill you?" Thea asked.

"He won't get the chance," Dick said tightly.

"How can you be so sure?"

"Because I'm going to kill him."

The sidewalks of Los Palabras were crowded with people out for an evening's entertainment when Dick and his team pulled up in front of the library. They marched up the front stairs, and after running right past the startled librarian, headed straight for the stairwell in the back of the building.

Dick was overwhelmed by a sense of déjà vu as he led his team up the tight stairs toward the roof. "Hold your fire until we see what we're dealing with," he called over his shoulder as their footsteps echoed off the concrete walls of the small space. "But be ready for anything."

They stopped at the door at the top of the stairs. Dick looked back at his team's anxious faces and hoped he didn't look as worried as they did.

"Ewan, Big, cover the left," Dick whispered. Ewan and Big nodded.

"Thea, Anna, cover the right. I've got the center. Set?"

They all nodded.

Dick reached into his pocket to grab the index cards and take a quick glance at them, but Thea reached out and held his wrist. He looked up at her, and she shook her head.

"No," she said softly. "You don't need them."

Dick thought for a moment and then lowered his hand, nodding. He tucked the cards back in his pocket, then turned back toward the door and kicked it open, transporting himself back in time.

The parapet that bordered the front wall of the building was piled high with stacks of paper. Standing in the dead center in front of the paper wall was Anton Nym, a gun held casually at his side. Next to him stood Doctor Paye. To their left were a pair of soldiers dressed exactly as the errorists had been that night, down to their camouflage uniforms, black Kevlar vests, and blank, mirrored face masks. Two more soldiers stood to their right.

"Richard!" Nym exclaimed in his distorted voice. "You made it! Brought your entire entourage, I see. How flattering."

Dick held his weapon at high port, trained directly at the asterisk in the center of Nym's forehead. His plan had been to gun down Nym the instant he saw him, but the stacks of paper gave him pause.

"Does this scene look at all familiar?" Nym spread his arms wide. "Is it ringing any bells?"

"How could you know about this?" Dick heard himself ask, the blood pulsing in his ears. "Everything about that night was classified."

"One just needs to know who to ask," Nym replied.

Dick took a few steps forward and felt his team move with him.

"Step away from the stacks of paper, get down on your knees, and put your hands behind your head," Dick commanded. He glanced at the soldiers on either side of Nym. "All of you! Now!"

"Do you mean these stacks of paper?" Nym asked innocently, patting the pile directly behind him so that it swayed ominously.

"Step away!" Dick repeated. "Now!"

"Or what?" Nym asked. "Surely you wouldn't shoot me or any of my associates and risk another . . . incident. Would you?"

Dick stood, frozen, his weapon still trained on Nym.

"Forgive my terrible manners," Nym said suddenly. "I haven't introduced you to my team."

He gestured to the soldier on the far right. The soldier holstered his gun, reached up, and removed his helmet. Only it didn't reveal a he, but a she.

"I believe you know Red Penny," Nym said. Penny shook out her auburn hair and smiled.

Nym gestured to the next soldier in line. He removed his helmet as Dick found himself looking at Scott Shwiski's face.

"Told you you'd see me again. *Dick*," Scott said.

Nym then turned with a flourish to the soldiers on his other side. He gestured to the one closest to him. The helmet came off and it was Elizabeth, the girl from Whey Cool. Dick was just processing what he was seeing when the final helmet came off, and he found himself looking into the face of Miss Information.

"My team," Nym said. " Can I assemble one or what?"

Dick pulled his attention back to Nym. "So they're going to show their faces, but you're not?" he asked. "Come on, Nym. We're all dying to know. Let's see that mug of yours."

Nym stared at Dick for a long time, seeming to deliberate. He looked at Doctor Paye, who, after a moment's hesitation, nodded. Nym turned back to Dick, and then stuck his thumbs under his mask to pull it up.

Dick had a number of theories about who Nym might be. But when the mask came off, he certainly never expected to be looking into Chicago's face.

"No," Dick whispered. "This isn't possible."

"Yes, Richard," Nym nodded. "I'm afraid it is."

"But they took you," Dick said, still trying to process what he was seeing. "At Fula Ord. I heard them kill you."

"That was actually a bit of theater," Nym said. "Those men work for me, you see. They brought me down the corridor and out of sight, and I made a loud fuss and all that, but really I was just getting changed into my . . . supervillain outfit? I wanted to cause you more suffering, thinking I was dead."

Dick was reeling.

"So your mental illness? Was that an act, too?"

"Oh, no, that was very real," Nym said. "I mean, obviously when I saw you earlier today, that was more theater. But I've actually been better for quite some time. I'd probably have spent the rest of my life shuffling around that place and talking to myself if it hadn't been for this extraordinary woman."

He stood, wrapped his arm around Doctor Paye's waist, and kissed her deeply.

"I don't understand."

"I've been working with some experimental treatments," Doctor Paye said. "Nothing that the hospital would ever sanction, but effective nonetheless. I was able to graft a brand-new personality onto your brother here. One that's highly intelligent, cunning, focused, and completely sane."

"It's like a personality transplant," Nym

said. "Imposed dissociative identity disorder, if you will. We created Anton Nym together, she implanted him in my brain, and eventually he took over and subsumed Chicago. So when I told you Chicago's death was necessary, I was being completely honest. Chicago's gone. And frankly, good riddance."

"Indeed," Doctor Paye said. "I can do the same for you, Dick. You and Anton can be partners in crime. The Brothers Nym."

"Oh, I like that!" Anton exclaimed. "What do you say, Dick? You could be Sinnon Nym. Or maybe Homo Nym?"

Despite the tense situation, Dick heard Big burst out laughing. "As if he doesn't get enough jokes about his name already," said Big.

"Chicago—" Dick began.

"Anton Nym," Chicago corrected him immediately.

"Anton Nym," Dick parroted irritably. "I'm not joining you. You're a murderer."

"How do you figure?" Nym was smiling now. "You intercepted the typo at Whey Cool, just as I knew you would. Same with the one at Strunk Field. You prevented my book from being released. I merely eliminated Chicago; I didn't kill him. You might charge me with attempted murder, but that's a very different animal."

Dick was staring at Nym disbelievingly. "What about Superscript? What about the two guards and those six CLITs at the Grammatica?"

Nym's smile faded and his eyelid began to twitch again. "What . . . what're you talking about?"

Doctor Paye stepped in front of Nym, putting her hands on his cheeks. "Don't listen to him, my love. He's trying to confuse you."

Dick pressed on. "Superscript was just twenty-one years old. The bullet you put in him went right through his heart. You killed him instantly."

Nym was now switching between looking at Dick and looking at Paye. A look of mingled horror and disgust spread across his face.

"You're not a killer, darling," Doctor Paye said soothingly. "You haven't killed anyone."

"Those two guards just inside the entrance to the Grammatica," Dick continued. "You splattered their brains all over the floor. And there's all those bodies at Fula Ord."

"It's a trick, my sweet, it's all a trick," Doctor Paye said rapidly. "You're completely sane now, you only deal in typos, and only to antagonize your brother for what he did to you."

Dick was eager to press his advantage, but he paused at her words. "What *I* did to him?"

Doctor Paye turned, looking straight at Dick. "Yes," she said. "Everything that happened to him was your fault."

"This," Dick said, gesturing to Nym, who now had both hands on the sides of his head as though trying to hold his brains in, "has nothing to do with me. This is your fault."

"I can't have killed anybody." Nym rubbed his temples.

"You were the one who talked him into joining Typo Squad in the first place," Doctor Pye said scornfully.

"Oh no," Dick said to Paye, smiling tightly. "Nice try, doc, but I'm through feeling guilty for that."

"I'm not a killer," Nym said, his voice more plaintive. Scott, Elizabeth, Penny, and Miss Information began to look uncomfortable and unsure.

Doctor Paye turned from Dick back to Nym. "Of course you're not, my love. Of course you're not. Your brother is just trying to manipulate you. Don't let him."

"*I'm* trying to manipulate him!" Dick cried, and without thinking took a step forward. He knew in an instant he'd made a mistake. Nym saw Dick's movement and immediately snapped back to his previous self.

"Stay where you are, Richard!" Nym shouted, stepping back and putting a hand on the nearest pile of flyers. "Don't move another inch."

Dick froze where he was. The brothers considered one another for a few moments.

"My people and I are leaving now, Richard," Nym said calmly.

"You know I can't let you do that," Dick said.

"You don't have a choice in the matter.

Unless you want to be responsible for another massacre."

Dick's eyes flicked over to Ewan and Big. They still had their weapons drawn and aimed, but they both looked back at him and gave almost imperceptible shakes of their heads. He looked over at Thea and Anna, who did the same.

As the team watched, Penny and Miss Information stepped slowly sideways, moved behind Nym and Doctor Paye, and squirmed through a gap between the two centermost piles of paper. Dick could just make out the railing of a fire escape beyond. Scott and Elizabeth followed suit, and Doctor Paye brought up the rear.

Nym bent down, grabbed his mask, and put it back on. He spread his arms wide.

"Well, it's been lovely spending time with you, dearest brother, but the future beckons," he said, his voice once again distorted. With a quick salute of his gun, Nym stepped backward into the gap.

"This isn't over!" Dick called after him.

Nym stopped and turned back. "My dear Richard," he said, smiling, "this has just barely begun." He stepped further back and disappeared.

The Typo Squad team lowered their weapons and exchanged glances. Big put his hand on Dick's shoulder.

"Don't worry, big guy," Big said. "We'll get him."

Dick nodded.

"All right, grab as many of those flyers as you can and pull them back from the edge," Dick commanded. But before any of them could take a single step, a series of small red lights began flashing on the ledge under the piles.

"The hell?" Dick said, and suddenly a series of small explosions went off along the parapet, and in a horrible slow motion, the piles of flyers tipped over the edge of the building and disappeared.

"No!" Dick shouted, running as fast as he could to the roof's edge, the rest of the team at his heels. Below them, the flyers floated and danced in the air as they spread all over Main

Street. Dick could see people below already looking up, pointing, and grabbing for the first arrivals.

He couldn't tear his gaze away as a young couple snatched two of the flyers out of the air and examined them. They looked curious for a moment, then tossed the flyer aside and went on their way.

"What's going on?" Dick asked quietly, as more people picked up the pieces of paper and nothing happened.

"Look!" Thea said, grabbing a fistful of flyers that had stayed behind. "They're blank!"

Dick snatched them out of her hand and flipped them over to see both sides. There was nothing written on them at all.

"Son of a bitch," Dick said. He scrambled over to another nearby pile of papers and checked them as well. Blank.

"It was a bluff," Thea said.

Dick scrambled to the fire escape. "Come on!" he shouted to the others as he swung around on the handrail and mounted the top set of stairs. "They can't be far!"

Rust shook from the structure as five sets

of boots thundered down to street level. Dick jumped down off the last catwalk and onto the crowded sidewalk, filled with pedestrians still trying to make sense of the blanket of paper that now covered the street. Thea, Big, Ewan, and Anna landed behind him.

"Big, right alleyway," Dick said quickly. "Anna, left alleyway. Ewan, Thea, the shops across the street."

The words were barely out of his mouth and the team ran off in the directions he'd indicated. Dick turned, considering the library. He mounted the steps and made his way through the double doors.

"Not you again!" the librarian cried as he made his way to her horseshoe-shaped desk in the library's main room.

"Sorry," Dick whispered, digging out his ID and badge and flashing it at her. She raised her reading glasses from her bosom, studied his credentials, and seemed satisfied. "Did anyone come through here in the past few minutes?"

"Several people have, gratefully," she whispered back. "So few people read anymore. It's encouraging."

"What I mean is," Dick whispered, "have you seen anyone unusual? Maybe a guy dressed all in black wearing a mask with a silver asterisk on the forehead?"

The librarian studied him. "Young man," she whispered at last, "perhaps you should be checked for a concussion."

Dick returned to the sidewalk a few minutes later, just in time to see the rest of the team regather.

"Anything?" Dick asked.

"No sign of them," Big said, sounding winded.

"Nothing," Anna said.

Thea and Ewan both shook their heads.

"All right," Dick said. "They can't have gotten out of Los Palabras yet. I'll call the LPPD and have them put out a BOLO on them."

He looked around at the sidewalk and the street beyond, both completely covered in pieces of paper. "I guess we'd better call the Department of Public Works, too. And tell them to bring a shit-ton of recycling bins."

Dick drove the team back to Typo Squad headquarters. He was exhausted and cranky, and could tell the others were as well. He muttered to himself as they made their way through the streets of Los Palabras.

"He played me, all right. He *knew* I'd go to Miss Information. Sent me to Fula Ord so I'd see him all weak and crazy, never suspect him. Sent me back to Mot Grange so he'd have time to kill everyone in the institution and set up the typo room. Made me believe that Nym was coming to get him so I'd rush back to Fula Ord with you guys and he'd be able to get the jump on us."

He whacked the steering wheel with his open palm.

"And I fell for it! All of it!"

"Dick," Thea said from the passenger seat, her hand to her eyes as though she had a headache. "Don't."

"Nym is in the wind for now," Anna said from behind him. "But we'll find him."

"Don't forget Paye," Dick said bitterly.

"She's the one who turned my brother into a typo-obsessed, murdering psychopath."

"She must have been the one taking him on his Anton Nym field trips from Fula Ord," Big said. "I bet she was even driving the limo outside the Grammatica."

"And she probably bankrolled the entire operation," Dick said. "Jesus."

"But if she put Anton Nym in Chicago's head," Thea said, "then she might be able to take him out too."

"Maybe," Dick said. "If she doesn't screw him up even worse in the meantime."

"Can you imagine how the paperwork on this is gonna read?" Big groused as they entered the lobby. "*Psycho with asterisk bindi blows up stacks of printer paper.*"

"When was the last time you filled out any paperwork?" Ewan asked.

"It's been known to happen," he replied.

They crossed the lobby and Dick spotted Autumn at her post behind the front desk.

"Autumn, if there was ever a night I needed to hear your crazy laugh," Dick sighed, "it's tonight."

It wasn't until they got close that they saw Autumn was weeping. Her mascara had run down her cheeks, creating dark tracks down to her chin.

Thea immediately ran to her and put a reassuring hand on Autumn's shoulder. "Honey," she said. "What is it?"

Autumn looked up at Dick, and answered Thea's question in a watery voice.

"Tanka's dead."

CHAPTER FOURTEEN

A cold, miserable rain fell from an iron sky as they all gathered in Los Palabras Cemetery to pay their respects to Sergeant Tanka.

Dick, Big, Ewan, Justin, and two of Tanka's nephews served as pallbearers. Dressed once again in their dress uniforms, they slid Tanka's casket out of the hearse and began a long walk through an honor guard to Tanka's final resting place.

As they made their way along through the gathering puddles, men and women on either side of the walkway snapped to attention and saluted. Dick noticed the insignia patches of dozens of typo organizations gathered to say farewell to one of their own: the Typo Rangers, out of Texas; the Typo Freedom

Fighters, with their distinctive stars-and-stripes insignia, from Boston; the Typo Enforcers from Chicago; and even members of the Escuadrón de Errores from Mexico City. Dick's heart was heavy, but the sight of all of those people who had traveled hundreds and in some cases thousands of miles to be there made him feel a bit better.

At the gravesite, the team stood huddled under black umbrellas in a vast crowd of black overcoats, suits, and dresses to say goodbye. Dick was sure that the priest was conveying words of comfort and solace, but none of them penetrated the unreality of burying Tanka. He turned to look at Thea. She was utterly disconsolate. He put an arm around her shoulders, pulling her close, rubbing her arm and choking back hot tears of his own.

After the service, Dick and Thea headed off toward the team's limo when they were approached by an older gentleman in full dress uniform. He was handsome, ramrod straight, and he carried himself with the utmost dignity.

"Dick," he said, extending his hand.

"Commander," Dick said, smiling as he shook the man's hand. "So glad you could come. Thea, this is Commander Reese Peck, the highest ranking officer in Typo Squad."

Thea shook his hand. "Very nice to meet you."

"And you, miss; and you."

"It was a beautiful service," Dick said.

"Yes, indeed it was," the Commander agreed. "I'll miss Tanka a great deal. I recruited him when he was not much older than this young lady right here."

"I didn't know that," Dick said.

"Yes, well, he was something of a private man, kept to himself. Still, an exceptional officer. If there's any glimmer of light in all this dreadful business, it's that he lost his life in the line of duty. That's as it should be."

"Yes, I suppose it is," Dick said.

"Look, I realize this is a difficult time for you—for all of you, really—but the fact remains that we have a dangerous killer still on the loose, and we need him brought to justice as fast as is humanly possible."

"Yes, sir," Dick said grimly. "I couldn't

agree more."

"I knew you'd feel that way, Dick," the Commander said. "So to move forward, I'm promoting you to lieutenant. Congratulations."

He extended his hand once again and Dick, thunderstruck, shook it.

"Congratulations, Dick," Thea said.

The shock slowly wore off and Dick came back to himself. "It's not the way I would've wanted it to happen, but I'm honored. Thank you, sir."

"You're entirely welcome," the Commander said. "I want Anton Nym apprehended and brought to justice. I've already spoken to the mayor. Whatever resources you need are at your disposal. Liaise with any other typo organizations you need to. Let's get this done."

"Yes, sir."

"Let me know if you need anything. A pleasure meeting you, Thea," the commander said. He tipped the brim of his hat, then moved off into the gathering gloom.

Big, Anna, and Autumn joined them.

"What was that all about?" Anna asked.

"He just promoted Dick to lieutenant," Thea said, trying to keep her gleeful tone subdued in the cemetery.

"Congratulations. Boss," Anna said with a smile.

"You're going to do a wonderful job, sweetie." Autumn got up on her tiptoes to kiss Dick's cheek.

"Yeah, well," Big said, making a show of putting out his hand to shake Dick's, "don't think I'm gonna salute you or anything."

"Thanks, guys," Dick said. He looked around. "Where's Ewan?"

The others looked around as well. Apparently they hadn't realized he wasn't with them.

"There he is," Big said, pointing to two men deep in conversation under a large tree a short distance away.

"Who's the other guy?" Autumn asked. "I don't recognize him."

"Look at his insignia," Dick said. The patch on the other man's shoulder was a circle of the deepest purple, with three golden fountain pen tips arranged in the shape of a crown. "He's from Her Majesty's Royal Typo Brigade."

"He came here from London?" Anna asked.

"Looks like it," Dick said. "Tanka was even more well-respected than I thought. Wonder what he wants with Ewan?"

A few moments later, the two men embraced, and Ewan made his way over to the team. He looked profoundly shaken.

"Everything all right?" Thea asked.

"Mmm?" Ewan said, composing himself. "Oh. Yes. Just . . . catching up with an old friend."

"Well you missed all the excitement," Big told him. "Commander Peck just made Dick lieutenant!"

A look of joy spread across Ewan's face. "How wonderful!" He patted Dick's arm. "A superb choice!"

"Thanks," Dick said.

"There's a memorial service over at The Galley," Autumn said. "We can toast Dick's promotion and raise a glass to Tanka. And I can get to know that one gentleman from the Typo Freedom Fighters. Did you see him? Tall handsome guy with a goatee?"

"Autumn!" Thea hissed, though she was smiling broadly. "This is a funeral!"

"So, what, I'm supposed to be blind just because we're in mourning?" Autumn protested. "I'm only human!"

Dick smiled as he and his team made their way back to the limo. They all piled in, but Dick stood by the open door. Thea leaned out. "Aren't you coming?"

Dick thought it over. "I'll meet you guys at The Galley. I just have to make a stop first."

Dick walked down to the end of Bartlett Pier, the rain finally giving way and the sky glowing a dull yellow over the rocky waters. There wasn't another soul to be seen, and Dick was fine with the solitude.

He reached the end of the pier and took a moment to breathe in the salt air and stare at the unbroken horizon. He raised his foot and rested it on a crossbar. He wondered why he didn't come here more often.

He reached into his jacket pocket and slowly pulled out his battered old index cards. He didn't read them, but regarded the backs of them and smiled at them like old friends. After a few moments, he tore them in half, then in half again, and again, and released the pieces to the wind, which carried them down to the water below.

No sooner did the last scrap touch the surface than his phone rang. "Yeah?"

"Hey, boss man!" Big's voice came through loud and clear, despite the crowd noise around it. "Where are you? You're missing all the free food. And there are some great Tanka stories floating around that you're not gonna want to miss."

Dick smiled. "I'm on my way. Don't put the lampshade on your head until I get there, okay?"

"Too late," Big said, and hung up.

Dick took one long, last look at the ocean and his phone rang again. "Hey, I said I'm on my way," Dick said.

"Are you certain you don't have anything else you wish to tear up and throw in the ocean?" Nym's mocking voice asked.

Dick unholstered his gun, looking around wildly. There were beaches on either side of the pier, but they were completely barren. He scanned the boardwalk at the other end of the pier, but all the stores and attractions were shuttered for the season.

"Don't give yourself a migraine," Nym said. "You shan't find me."

"Maybe not today," Dick said, still scanning in every direction. "But trust me, I will."

"Richard, I'm calling to convey something important, so please pay attention."

Dick focused his attention on his phone. "I'm listening."

"Do you recall the library rooftop, when I explained to you how the beautiful and talented Doctor Paye had given me my new personality?"

"Yeah," Dick said.

"Well one thing I neglected to mention is that my new personality is completely immune to the effects of typos," Nym said.

"Yeah, well, I figured as much," Dick said.

"Otherwise your mass-murdering schemes might've accidentally killed you."

"Too true!" Nym said. "And I have far too much to do to allow that to happen. You see, I'm recruiting, Richard. Penny and Shwiski and Elizabeth and Miss Information were just the beginning. I'm amassing an army."

Dick felt himself go cold. "An army?"

"Yes. You see, Doctor Paye's technique can work on anyone. So I'm gathering up the poor, the forgotten, the disenfranchised, and I'm having them . . . indoctrinated with my ideology. And at the same time, I'm making them all immune to typos."

A horrible, dawning realization took hold, and Dick felt his mouth go dry. "You're creating an errorist cell."

"Precisely!" Nym sounded delighted. "The biggest errorist cell in history. There will be no stopping us, Richard. So I implore you not to try."

"Why are you telling me this?" Dick asked.

"Because you're still, on some level, my brother. And truthfully, I don't want you to get hurt."

"I've got to come after you, Nym," Dick said quietly. "You know that."

"Then come," Nym said. "And die."

The phone went dead. Dick could feel his pulse pounding in his ears. He looked up Thea's number and called her.

"Hey!" she said, the same crowd noise behind her that had been behind Big. "Are you coming down or what?"

"Listen, gather everyone and meet me at headquarters as soon as possible," Dick said quickly.

"What?" Thea said. "Why?"

"Because we're going to war," Dick said, and hung up.

ALSO AVAILABLE BY STEPHEN LOMER

Stargazer Lilies or Nothing at All

JOIN TYPO SQUAD TODAY!

Visit **www.typo-squad.com**
to join our ranks and pick up some
cool Typo Squad merchandise
to show your pride!

The best way you can show your support for an author—besides buying and enjoying his or her books, of course—is to post a review on amazon.

If you enjoyed *Typo Squad*, please post a review today. Thank you!

ABOUT THE AUTHOR

Stephen Lomer has been writing books, novellas, short stories, and scripts for nearly a decade, and one or two of them are actually pretty good. A grammar nerd, *Star Trek* fan, and other things that chicks dig, Stephen is the creator, owner, and a regular contributor to the website Television Woodshed. He's a hardcore fan of the Houston Texans, despite living in the Hub of the Universe his whole life, and believes Mark Twain was correct about pretty much everything.

Stephen lives on Boston's North Shore with his wife, Teresa.

Made in the USA
Middletown, DE
15 July 2017